Cry for Help

Books by Doris Miles Disney

Cry for Help

DORIS MILES DISNEY

PUBLISHED FOR THE CRIME CLUB BY
DOUBLEDAY & COMPANY, INC.
GARDEN CITY, NEW YORK
1975

All of the characters in this book are fictitious, and any resemblance to actual persons, living or dead, is purely coincidental.

Library of Congress Cataloging in Publication Data

Disney, Doris Miles.
    Cry for help.

    I. Title.
PZ3.D626Cr [PS3507.I75]   813'.5'2
ISBN 0-385-03441-5
Library of Congress Catalog Card Number 74–14377

For the Michigan Club—
foes over pennies at cards
but always good friends

Cry for Help

CHAPTER ONE

"Hot Line, this is Martha," Rachel Carey said. "Can I help you?"

"Uh . . . do I have to tell you my name, ma'am?" asked a young male voice still in the process of changing.

"No, not at all."

"Oh." Relief softened the squeaky note. "That's what I was told but I wanted to be sure. Happens I've got this health problem . . ."

"Yes?"

A pause, a fresh start. "It's something I wouldn't want my parents to find out about . . ."

"Yes?" Rachel said again encouragingly, aware of what was to come.

"Happens, you see, there's this girl in school . . . She's been, well, fooling around with a lot of different guys—if you know what I mean, ma'am?"

"I think so."

"Well, I kind of got mixed up with her myself. And now I've got these funny little symptoms that I've been kind of worried about lately. I didn't want to say anything about them to anyone but then today I got talking to this older guy—he's a senior—and he said I'd better check it out."

"That seems like a good idea."

"Thing is, though, I can't go to our family doctor. He'd tell my parents and they'd have fits. They'd end up taking away all my privileges, including the car."

The young voice was steadier now that the problem was

out in the open and there was no reaction of shock or censure in Rachel's response to it.

"Especially the car, because they'd figure that if I hadn't had the use of it, maybe the girl and I . . ."

"That is a point," Rachel agreed.

"So I wondered if there was some way I could have a medical examination without having my parents find out about it."

"Yes, there is a way. The City Health Department." Rachel spun the circular file on the desk around to Health. "Shall I give you their phone number?"

"Oh yes. But—do you know how much it costs?"

"It's free." Rachel read off the number.

When it was written down the young voice said hesitantly, "I'm not of age, you know. Only sixteen. Are you sure, ma'am, they won't tell my parents if it turns out that I—well—that I've got—what I think I have?"

"Yes, I'm sure they won't."

"Gee, that's great. Thanks an awful lot, ma'am."

"You're welcome. Good luck."

Rachel's tone was cordial but she shook her head ruefully as she hung up. They were getting younger and younger, the kids with problems. Any day now she wouldn't be a bit surprised to have an eighth grader on the phone worried about VD. Just last week one of the aides had had a call from a ninth grader who was on hard drugs.

She filled out a daily sheet on the call, putting down the time, 8:55 P.M.; category, VD; sex, male; age, sixteen; referral, City Health Department. Under remarks she wrote, "Boy concerned that parents might find out about his possible condition."

Rachel signed it with her code name Martha, tore the sheet off the pad and added it to those already made out since her shift had begun at eight o'clock. It ran until midnight; three hours to go.

She hoped they would be as busy as the first hour.

When the phone kept ringing the time passed quickly; when there were fewer calls she was sometimes aware of the quiet, the sense of isolation in the old house, hemmed in by commercial buildings that were all in darkness at night. In the house itself there were other offices, a small loan company across the hall, an estate auctioneer and a public accountant upstairs, but they too were mostly in darkness at night.

Hot Line occupied two rooms, what had once been the dining room when the house was a private residence and the kitchen, left much as it was except for a bathroom partitioned off it. The office was furnished with a desk, filing cabinets, a few chairs and a cot bed for the aide who took over from midnight until eight in the morning. There was no identification on the double-locked door opening into the front hall; anonymity was an essential part of Hot Line's work.

The phone rang, a wrong number. It rang again just as Rachel finished making a record of the wrong number call. The girl on the line, a teen-ager, had a straightforward problem; she needed eyeglasses that her parents couldn't afford to buy. "So my mother said maybe Hot Line would know where I could get free ones," the girl concluded.

"Lions Club might be able to help you," Rachel said, spinning the file around to listings under Eyes. "Would you like the number? You can call it any day after five o'clock."

"Oh yes."

Rachel read off the number.

"Thank you very much," the girl said writing it down.

"You're welcome."

There was a lull after that. Rachel, who covered Hot Line Tuesdays and Fridays, found time to read a note on the bulletin board asking for someone to swap around and take the Thursday night shift from eight to twelve.

There was no reason she couldn't do it. She reached for the second phone on the desk, an unlisted number for the use of the aides, and called Mrs. Powell, the chairman of volunteers, to arrange the substitution.

The lull continued. Rachel opened the book she had brought with her but almost at once the phone rang.

"Hot Line, this is Martha," she said. "Can I help you?"

"I don't know if you can or not but I'm just about at the end of my rope." It was a woman calling, her voice heavy with despair. "My husband drinks all the time. He come home a little while ago from some bar he was at—don't matter which, he knows them all—since he got out of work at four o'clock. Couldn't hardly walk and how he drove home I don't know. Didn't want no supper, gave me a slap on the mouth when I said he should eat something and went up to bed. He's sleeping it off now. Kids was crying—I don't know what to do."

"Has it been going on very long?" Rachel asked.

"He always drank some but it's getting worse and worse. We don't have no decent home life, our kids, they're afraid of him. He's always knocking us around. I don't know which way to turn."

"Oh, that's too bad." Rachel paused. "Have you ever talked to him about joining AA—Alcoholics Anonymous?"

"Plenty of times. He just gets mad, says he don't need it. Says he could stop drinking any time he felt like it but why should he. Only pleasure he's got, he says. So you see . . ." The woman sighed deeply.

Rachel checked the file under Alcoholism. Listed were Alcoholics Anonymous, Alcoholic Treatment Center, Al-Anon.

She thought for a moment. The resigned hopeless note in the woman's voice indicated that she wasn't prepared to separate from her husband or seek legal counseling.

"Have you ever thought of joining Al-Anon yourself?" she asked.

"What's that?"

"It's a group similar to AA except that it's for people who have to live with an alcoholic."

"What do they do?"

"They get together and talk over problems they have with the drinking member of their family, how they handle them and so forth. The idea is that by sharing their experiences they're able to help each other."

"Oh. Do they have regular meetings?"

"Yes, they do." Rachel hesitated wanting to add, Why don't you try it? But as a volunteer, her only function was to make referrals, not to give advice or counseling herself.

After a moment she said, "I have the Al-Anon phone number here if you'd like to have it. Then when you've had time to think it over, you can decide whether or not you want to call them."

"Just a minute till I get a pencil."

The woman wrote down the phone number. "Maybe I will call them, at that," she said. "Wouldn't do no harm and might do some good."

"Well, if you call them, I hope it does," Rachel replied.

The woman thanked her and hung up.

Rachel made out a daily sheet on the call and sat back in her chair feeling suddenly depressed. Dealing with drinking problems tended to have that effect on her. They were all basically the same, regardless of individual backgrounds. There had been a time when her despair over her own husband's drinking had almost led her to join Al-Anon herself. The only thing that kept her from it was her awareness that for her it would just be a postponement of decision.

A year ago last summer that decision was reached. After four years of marriage, with the situation getting worse instead of better, she left Neil and was now in the process of divorce.

The phone was silent for quite some time. Rachel opened her book, trying to put painful thoughts of her husband out of her mind. Then restlessness brought her to her feet and out into the kitchen to make herself a cup of instant coffee.

The phone was still silent as she drank it wandering around the room with her coffee cup in her hand. She glanced at the double-locked back door. Was the night still as mild as if it were April instead of early February?

She unlocked the door and went out onto the back porch. It was a beautiful night, the air soft, the stars brilliant overhead. She stood there finishing her coffee, looking out at the small parking lot intended for the use of the tenants. Her car was the only one in it.

She walked to the end of the porch and there had an oblique view of Lafayette Inn across the street where legend said the French general had spent the night during his triumphal American tour in 1824. Bright lights shone from the inn. The sound of dance music reached her faintly from the Yorktown Room. There must be a party going on there tonight, she thought.

A party. She hadn't been to one, not a real party, since she left Neil.

She shook off the thought—self-pity was an unlovely trait —and went back inside.

The night wore on. A call from a working mother, new in town, about nursery schools; a call asking what could be done about a neighbor's cat that howled half the night; a call seeking information on treatment for a retarded child.

There were daily sheets for ten calls by eleven o'clock and only one after that from an old lady who insisted that Hot Line should be able to get Monmouth City Council to put in a brighter street light on her corner.

At quarter of twelve Rachel got up from the desk, took a good stretch and walked around the room halting in front of the mirror over the boarded-up fireplace to comb her dark thick cap of hair worn in an expensively casual cut. She looked pale, she thought. She hadn't slept well last night. There were too many nights like that, troubled with doubts and questions about both the past and the future.

She took out her lipstick, put it back. Why bother at this hour when she was going straight home? Silly. Or maybe it wasn't. She took it out again and applied it carefully.

The aides' coded knock sounded on the hall door.

"Yes?" Rachel said.

"It's me, Susan Crowe," came the cheery answer.

Rachel opened the door smiling at the newcomer as she greeted her.

Everyone smiled at Susan Crowe whose own quick smile and friendly approach had that effect on people.

"So how'd it go?" she inquired.

"Fine."

"My old man dropped me off," said Susan referring to her husband who worked the midnight shift at a local plant. "My car's gone on the blink again."

"Oh, too bad."

Susan laughed. "No, it's not. Finally got him to agree it's time I had a new one. Look, I'll watch from the kitchen window till you leave. Our landlord really should put a better light out there than that feeble little thing by the back porch. Seems to me it gets dimmer all the time."

"Maybe it's because the stars are so bright tonight," Rachel suggested as she put on her coat and gathered up her belongings.

She couldn't go out the kitchen door to the parking lot. The steps had been removed and the whole back porch railed in long ago.

She said good night and went out into the front hall where the ceiling light lost itself in the dark wood paneling and the shadows of the staircase.

Susan stood at the kitchen window, waving and smiling as Rachel drove out of the parking lot.

She lived in a garden apartment only a few minutes away. Following familiar turns along the quiet streets she was once again conscious of how tired she was tonight. She would go right to bed and try not to let unhappy thoughts keep her awake. She would be much better off if she could change her attitude, become more like Susan Crowe, more inclined to look on the bright side of things.

After all, she was still fairly young, not thirty yet; she wasn't short of money, she could leave Monmouth and go back to full-time teaching once her divorce went through; there must be lots of good things still ahead for her.

CHAPTER TWO

Celia Hotchkiss, Rachel's sister, called her the next afternoon. They were very close in age, only eighteen months apart, the two adventurous members of their family, who had come east from Lexington, Kentucky to attend the University of Pennsylvania. Rachel, the older, qualifying first to teach, had got a job in Alexandria, Virginia. Celia had joined her there in the same school where she still taught and they had shared an apartment until Rachel married Neil Carey and moved thirty-five miles away to Monmouth. Celia, married now herself to a young lawyer in the Justice Department, lived in the same complex where she and Rachel had lived together over six years ago.

The difference was that Celia's marriage had turned out well. Her husband Bob was a solid dependable person, devoted to Celia.

There were sometimes twinges of pain for Rachel, the sense of having missed out on the normal pattern of life, in listening to their plans and seeing how happy they were together. But she kept these feelings to herself while Celia congratulated her on adjusting so well to her impending divorce.

Celia's major concern over her sister was that she didn't move back to Alexandria where they could see more of each other. Lethargy, Celia said, was all that kept Rachel in her Monmouth apartment, rented when she separated from Neil and they sold their house. It wasn't, Celia said, as if Rachel had any real ties in Monmouth.

Rachel did not admit that there was more than lethargy

involved in her reluctance to move away. It made no sense, she knew, that the finality implied in the move disturbed her. The real break had come the day she first went to a lawyer. But still, the reluctance was there, the memory of how happy she was when she and Neil, back from their honeymoon in Spain, settled in Monmouth in the house his father gave them for a wedding present.

With Celia she pleaded the convenience of being near her lawyer and the fact that her divorce would come up in Monmouth Municipal Court.

Only the divorce itself, when it was granted, would give her the impetus, she realized, to start a new life somewhere else.

Celia was calling that afternoon to invite her to dinner the next night. "They were having a special on rib roasts yesterday at Safeway," she said. "I picked up a real nice one and I thought you might like to share it with us."

"I'd love to but I can't," Rachel told her. "I'm swapping shifts with a girl on Hot Line tomorrow night. I said I'd take her place and she'll take mine Friday night instead."

Celia and Rachel's father-in-law were the only people who knew about her volunteer work on Hot Line. It was Celia, as her closest family connection, who had the unlisted Hot Line number to call in case of an emergency.

"Oh." Celia thought for a moment and said, "Well, there's no reason the rib roast can't sit in the refrigerator for another day. If you can come Friday night we'll have it then."

"That's fine with me. In fact, as long as I'm going to, I think I'll drive up early in the afternoon and do some shopping. I'll plan to get to your place around five or so."

"Okay, see you then." Celia said good-by and hung up.

Rachel finished her shopping in Alexandria about four-thirty that Friday afternoon but when she got back to her car at the parking lot where she had left it, it wouldn't start. She knew why the moment she heard the dull sound that meant a dead battery. Although the weather had cleared up since, it had still been raining when she left Monmouth and she had turned on her headlights, forgetting to turn them off when she arrived at the parking lot.

"Damn it all, how stupid of me," she muttered to herself, and got out of her car looking around for a phone booth to call a service station.

It turned out that she didn't have to. A young man parking his car next to hers came over and said, "Dead battery, eh?"

"Yes. I went off and left the lights on—of all things to do!"

He smiled over the exasperated note in her voice. "No great problem," he said. "Look, maybe the attendant here has a jump cable. I'll go ask him."

"Oh, thank you."

Rachel watched him walk away with a confident, long-legged stride, a very good-looking young man, blond and blue-eyed, with a well-groomed appearance.

He came back after conferring with the attendant and announced, "He's got one around here somewhere, he says. He'll go look for it when he's checked out a couple of cars that are ready to leave."

"Did he say he'd charge my battery for me?" Rachel asked.

"He's pretty busy. I said I would."

"Oh, but really—I didn't expect you to do it. It's an imposition—"

He grinned at her. "Okay, you've made the appropriate noises and now you can relax, Miss—?"

"Carey," she said and after a moment of hesitancy, "Mrs. Carey."

"Oh." His glance went to her ringless left hand. "I'm Luke Welford. Lucas, actually, but no one, thank God, calls me that—except for a great-aunt. Just last month when I was home over Christmas and we were at her house for dinner, I heard it. 'Lucas, why don't you give up smoking? So bad for your health and such a dirty habit too.' That's what really bothers her. The ash trays getting used. She's one of the ultra-clean types."

Rachel laughed. "I know someone like that. You hardly dare sit down for fear of wrinkling the cushions."

"Speaking of cigarettes . . ." He brought out a pack and offered one to her.

She shook her head. "No thanks, I finally managed to quit last year. Not because of dirty ash trays, though. The way I smoked, I was starting to get a morning cough."

"What self-discipline," he commented lighting a cigarette. "I'm afraid I don't have it. You live in Alexandria?"

"No, Monmouth. Just here shopping and then to my sister's for dinner."

He was studying her openly, liking what he saw, a slim young woman, perhaps five-six, with dark hair shorter than his own and lovely expressive dark eyes. Not pretty, he decided, features too strong for that, but bones that would outlast prettiness and a certain touch of elegance as well.

Mrs. Carey. But no wedding ring.

Rachel didn't mind the inspection, not when his approval was as open as his scrutiny.

The attendant brought over the jump cable and watched with indolent interest while Luke Welford connected it with his car battery and then with hers.

"Now get in and start your motor," he instructed her.

Almost immediately it rumbled back to life. She left it running and got out. "Black magic," she said with a smile. "Completely beyond me."

"Nothing to it." His smile was touched with masculine indulgence as he disconnected the jump cable.

The attendant waited while Rachel fished a dollar bill out of her pocketbook and handed it to him. "Thank you for letting me use it," she said.

The attendant nodded, took the cable and walked away.

She turned back to Luke Welford. "I can't tell you how

much I appreciate this," she began. "I don't know what I'd have done—"

"There's one way you can express appreciation," he broke in to suggest. "Let me buy you a drink. There's a place just down the street."

"Well . . ." After the briefest hesitation she said, "How nice. I'd love it."

They walked down the street to the cocktail lounge, still relatively deserted at a few minutes before five. He ordered a martini, Rachel, Scotch and water.

When their drinks were served they began exchanging information about themselves. Rachel learned that he worked for an advertising agency in Washington and had an apartment in one of the new complexes that were springing up in Alexandria; and that he came from Scranton, Pennsylvania and had attended George Washington University which led, after graduation, to his settling in the area.

"Scranton," she said. "I don't think I've ever been there." She paused for thought. "I'm not quite sure what part of Pennsylvania it's in."

"You're not alone in that," he told her. "I'm always running into people who, when I say it's my home town, act as if they're not certain it exists." His voice took on a mock-plaintive tone. "I can't think why. After all, over a hundred thousand people live there—including the ex-governor."

"Still, you left it," Rachel reminded him.

"And what place did you leave?"

"Lexington, Kentucky."

She went on to tell him a little bit about her background, her parents and three brothers still living in Lexington, the move east to college and then on to teaching that she and Celia had made.

She looked at her watch at the end of the recital. "Lord, it's almost five-thirty. Celia will be wondering what's keeping me."

"But we're just starting to get acquainted," Luke Welford

protested. "How about another drink? We'll make it a quick one."

"I really mustn't." Reluctant in her firmness, Rachel gathered up her pocketbook and gloves. It had been a pleasant interlude but it was better not to prolong it, this chance encounter, this pickup. And Celia expected her to arrive any minute.

"Well then, will you take a rain check on that second drink?" He signaled the waitress to bring the check.

She looked at him quizzically. "I don't see why not."

"Good."

They walked back to the parking lot. As he waited to make sure her car would start he asked, "May I call you sometime soon?"

"Yes. I'm listed as R. Carey in the phone book." He was probably wondering about her marital status, Rachel thought, but made no mention of it. He might never follow up this meeting. If he did, it would be soon enough to make some reference to it.

She hoped she would hear from him. She had gone out very little since her separation from Neil, feeling hesitant about it, even though her lawyer had explained to her that a legal separation gave her that freedom.

It was time she changed her attitude, she told herself saying good-by to Luke Welford. If he called she would go out with him. She had enjoyed his company. His interest had given her a small lift.

But she didn't bring up the incident during dinner with her sister and brother-in-law. Celia would want to know later on if she heard from him and if he didn't call she might as well keep her sense of letdown to herself.

That Sunday morning, however, Luke Welford called. He went straight to the point. "Any chance, on this short notice, that you'd be able to have dinner with me today?"

"Oh, I'm sorry but I've already made plans."

"Competition, huh?"

"I'd hardly call it that," Rachel said, as direct as he was. "My father-in-law is taking me out to dinner."

"Oh. Well, I won't suggest tomorrow. Monday's never my best day—but how about Tuesday night?"

Tuesday night, though, was Hot Line. "Oh dear, we're not having any luck, are we?" she said. "What about Wednesday or Thursday? Either one would be fine with me."

He wasn't free Wednesday. They settled on six-thirty Thursday night and he went on to ask directions to her apartment.

"You know the way into Monmouth from the exit on 95?"

"Yes, I know the route."

Rachel told him how to get to her apartment from downtown Clarence Street off 617. He knew where it was and seemed equally familiar with other streets she mentioned.

After she hung up Rachel wondered how he happened to know Monmouth so well. A local girl he had dated or was still dating?

It was none of her business.

Her father-in-law, Arthur Carey, a retired widower living alone in a historic old house in Prince William County, arrived to take her out to dinner at six o'clock that evening. Tall and stooped, with a beaky nose and white hair, at seventy he looked every bit of his age and more. He had married late and was nearing forty when Neil, his only child, was born.

His son's drinking had been a source of anxiety to him long before Neil met Rachel. Arthur Carey had hoped for a miracle when they were married and for the first year or two there had been some grounds for that hope but after that for another two years he had watched helplessly the disintegration of the marriage.

He and Rachel had grown very fond of each other, so close that she had talked over with him her decision to divorce Neil before she made the first move in that direction. He could not advise her against it or find it in himself to blame her, knowing how hard she had tried to make the marriage work. After the separation, the affectionate relationship between them had continued virtually unchanged.

His heavy white mustache brushed her cheek in a kiss when she opened the door for him. "Well, my dear," he greeted her.

When he was seated in the living room she made them each a drink, not needing to ask what he would have. It was always bourbon and water.

They talked about how fast the mild weather of the past week was changing.

"There's a real bite in the air tonight," he said. "You'll need a warm coat when we go out."

Rachel smiled, settling herself on the sofa opposite him. "I'll wear my mink."

He nodded with a pleased look. It was his Christmas gift to her the first year of her marriage.

They talked, taking their time over their drinks, and had a second one. "Everything all right with you, Rachel?" he asked presently, concerned as always with her welfare.

"Everything's fine, thank you."

"If you need any money—?"

"No indeed. You've been more than generous already."

As he had been, insisting on giving her ten thousand dollars over a year ago to supplement the division of money worked out by her husband's lawyer and hers when their house was sold.

Also, Rachel knew, her father-in-law had it in mind to make some sort of final settlement on her when the divorce went through. It was to give her a fresh start, he said, and to show his appreciation that she hadn't used Neil's drinking against him in the divorce proceedings. Many wives, he said, who had put up with as much as she had, would not have been so forbearing.

He took her to the Monmouth Inn for dinner. "Neil called

me last night," he said during the meal. "Florida's having a bad season, he was telling me. Nothing like the usual flood of tourists."

"The gas shortage, the papers say."

"Not just the motels and restaurants. Neil says the real estate business is suffering too."

"How is he?"

Arthur Carey shot a quick glance at her from under shaggy white brows. "Missing you, of course. He asked me if I thought there was any hope that you'd change your mind about the divorce."

Rachel looked at him without expression and said, "I hadn't told you but he called me last week and asked the same thing. But he knows and I know that it isn't any use." She came to a halt but then, thinking it would be no kindness to her father-in-law to encourage any flickering hope of his son's reform, she added, "He'd been drinking when he called me. Quite a lot, I'm afraid."

Arthur Carey sighed and shook his head. There was nothing more to say.

CHAPTER THREE

The girl called the following Tuesday night.

Rachel picked up the phone and glanced at the clock on the wall facing her. It was nine twenty-five. She wrote it down as she said, "Hot Line, this is Martha. Can I help you?"

"Just Martha—no last name?"

"Just Martha."

"Do I have to tell you my name?"

"No, it's not necessary."

"Oh." It was a rather light voice, educated tone, slightly breathless quality to it. "People could make up names, anyway, couldn't they?"

"If they wanted to. But there's no need of it."

"Don't you make some sort of a record, though, of people who call?"

"Yes, a brief one."

The girl—from her voice Rachel assumed she was no more than eighteen or nineteen—was silent until Rachel asked again, "Is there some way I can help you?"

The girl said then, "I don't know that I have what you'd call a problem exactly. It's just that I'm—well, I'm nervous tonight. I didn't want to call anyone I know and I've read about Hot Line so I thought I'd call."

The girl paused and then went on in a rush of words, "I'm alone in the house, you see. My husband's out—nothing unusual about that," an undercurrent of resentment. "He has this stupid teaching schedule, classes two nights a week, Tuesdays and Fridays (like her own Hot Line shifts, Rachel thought irrelevantly), and leaves me here alone. And tonight, just a few minutes ago when I went out with the rubbish, there was a man in our yard. One minute I saw him and the next he just seemed to disappear. I ran inside, turned out the lights and looked out one window after another, but I couldn't see him. We have lots of shrubbery, though, all around the yard, so that all he had to do was drop back into it."

"It couldn't have been a shadow, a branch moving in the wind?"

"No, but that's what my husband will probably say when he gets home. My imagination, he'll tell me." Again the undercurrent of resentment came through in the girl's voice. "But it's not. There was a man out in back. Fairly tall. I saw his silhouette quite clearly for a moment."

"Do you live here in the city or out in one of the counties?" Rachel inquired.

"Here but on the outskirts where the houses aren't close to each other. Oh, there's my doorbell." The girl sounded frightened. "It's sort of late for anyone to come calling. Would you mind holding on, Martha, while I go see who it is?"

"Not at all."

Rachel waited holding the receiver to her ear. She could hear the girl's voice faint in the distance calling, "Who is it? Who's there?"

No one seemed to answer. Presently she returned to the phone and said on a shaky note, "No one was there. It was the back door—two chimes—but no one was there."

Two chimes, Rachel thought. Shouldn't she have heard them too? She had been able to hear the girl's voice at the door and usually, talking to anyone when their doorbell rang, she could hear it.

"I went to the front door too just to make sure," the girl continued, "but no one was there. Whoever it was is still out there, though. Must be, ringing the bell like that."

She paused. Then she said, "It scares me stiff. My mother,

you see, was killed by a prowler three years ago last fall. Before I was married."

"How awful," Rachel said. "No wonder you're nervous. But why don't you call the police if you think there's someone outside?"

"What do you mean, if I think?" the girl demanded sharply. "Somebody rang my doorbell."

"Well then, call the police right away."

"I will." The girl hung up abruptly.

An odd little business, Rachel reflected as she hung up herself. A bit different from the usual run of calls. Was there really a prowler or was it, as she had suggested, a shadow, a branch moving in the wind?

But the wind didn't ring doorbells—if it really had rung. There'd been that resentment in the girl's voice over her husband's teaching at night . . . What if she was just making it all up, crying wolf, as it were, to get back at him for leaving her home alone?

And, in any case, if there was a prowler, why not call the police immediately instead of Hot Line? That was what most people would do—above all, anyone whose mother had been killed by one.

No answer to these questions. Rachel turned her attention to the call sheet she had started on the girl.

The phone rang. This time it was an older woman's voice and a query all too familiar; a son in high school had admitted to her that he was taking drugs.

Rachel referred her to the drug center, giving her the phone number.

Only eleven years ago when she was graduated from high school herself, marijuana had been the in thing.

Half an hour later the girl called her again.

"Well, Martha, the police have come and gone since I talked with you before," she announced without preliminary. "One policeman, that is. He looked all around outside but no prowler. He took off, of course, when the cruiser arrived."

"The whole yard was searched?"

"I reckon so, the length of time it took. No sign of anyone, the cop said. He just told me to keep my doors and windows locked—they were already—and to call again if whoever it was came back. Oh, and that he'd keep an eye on the house while patrolling the area."

The girl's flat tone indicated her dissatisfaction.

"Well, I really don't know what else he could do," Rachel said. "At least anyone who was around was scared off. I doubt you'll have any more trouble tonight."

"No, I don't expect to. My husband should be home soon, anyway. That is, unless he stays on talking to one of his students. He seems to have all the time in the world to give to them."

Resentment once again in the girl's voice. Rachel felt sorry for the husband. The girl would probably give him a hard time when he got home, making it all his fault that she had been frightened.

"I'd better hang up now," the girl said. "I wouldn't want him to arrive and find me talking with you. He thinks I'm nuts—or at least terribly neurotic—as it is. He says I tend to imagine things, dwell too much on the past and what happened to my mother."

"Well . . ." Rachel said with no particular inflection because there was nothing else she could say.

"Thank you, though, Martha," the girl's voice softened, "for being so patient about listening. It helped."

"I'm glad it did. Good night."

"Good night, Martha."

Rachel filled out another daily sheet on the girl, went out into the kitchen to make a cup of coffee and carried it back to the desk.

The coffee was scalding hot. Rachel thought about the girl while she took cautious sips of it. Neurotic, she had called herself—or rather, said that was what her husband said she was, dwelling too much on the past and what had happened to her mother.

Assuming it was true—many tales told on Hot Line were not—that the mother had been killed by a prowler three years ago and that it had happened in Monmouth or the vicinity, it must have been reported in the Monmouth *Register* at the time, although Rachel herself had no recollection of reading about it. But then there were so many violent crimes in the news that all but the most recent ones tended to blur and run together in the mind.

If it had happened locally, she might be able to check on it in the back files at the newspaper office or in the library. Not that Rachel had any intention of doing it; Hot Line callers had every right to remain anonymous.

The rest of her shift was quiet. She finished reading the copy of *American Heritage* she had brought along before Susan Crowe arrived to take over from her at midnight.

Luke Welford arrived promptly at six-thirty Thursday evening. He was even better-looking than she'd remembered, Rachel thought, his blond good looks set off by a brown checked jacket, lighter brown slacks, pale gold shirt and brown and gold patterned tie.

Study in muted browns and golds, she thought, making mental comparisons with her husband's appearance the last few months they were together when he no longer cared what he wore or how he looked.

"Did you have any trouble finding me?" she asked as she led the way into the living room.

"Not a bit. Came straight as a homing pigeon."

She lived on an out-of-the-way residential street. He must be very familiar with Monmouth to have found it so easily. But she still didn't ask if he had friends there.

He stood in the doorway looking around appreciatively at the long living room that ran the full width of the apartment with a sliding glass door opening onto a balcony at one end.

It was an inviting room, furnished with a pleasant blend of old and new, a deep comfortable sofa and chairs Rachel had bought herself and family pieces of the Careys that her father-in-law had urged upon her when she and Neil broke up housekeeping.

"Nice," Luke Welford said. "Very nice, Mrs. Carey. Only I'd rather say Rachel."

She smiled. "Why don't you then? Shall we have a drink before we leave?"

"Fine. Scotch on the rocks, please."

"All right. Sit down while I get it."

Instead, he followed her out into the hall that led to the kitchen and dining ell on one side and the bedroom and bath on the other. "Can't I do it?" he said. "I wouldn't feel right letting a helpless female fix my drink."

Rachel raised an eyebrow as she opened the refrigerator to take out ice cubes. "Is that the way I look to you, Luke Welford?"

His smile came. It was charming. That's what he was anyway, she thought. A charmer.

But when he spoke he adopted a rueful tone. "Truth is, you look all too capable of taking care of yourself."

"That doesn't sound like a compliment," she countered.

"Wasn't meant to be," he said briskly.

And so, with laughter, the drinks were made.

He took her to dinner at the Monmouth Inn where Arthur Carey had taken her Sunday night, asking if that would suit her and finding his way there with the same ease that had brought him to her apartment.

Just another example of his familiarity with Monmouth, Rachel thought.

They were seated in the same section of the dining room as Sunday night, served by the same elderly, coffee-colored waiter.

He knew Rachel well. He greeted her with a warm, "How are you tonight, Miz Carey?" and flicked a measuring glance at her companion.

"Fine, Richard, thank you," Rachel replied as he seated her. "How's that leg of yours?" He still limped slightly from a car accident three months ago.

"Pretty good," he said. "Pretty good. But like I told old Mr. Carey Sunday when he was complainin' he couldn't see the menu like he used to, we ain't gettin' any younger, either one of us."

"Neither am I," Rachel said. "Nobody is. Sad fact of life."

"Too true, Miz Carey. You folks like a drink before you order?"

"By all means," Luke said.

When their drinks were brought he sat turning his glass between his hands and asked presently, "Old Mr. Carey is your father-in-law, Rachel?"

"Yes. He lives alone out in the county. His wife is long dead."

"Oh." It was voiced as a comment but his look was questioning.

Rachel said, "My husband and I are legally separated, Luke, and will be divorced late this summer. It's one of those no-fault-type divorces that require two years' separation."

"Oh," he said again.

He left it there, just looking at her, their glances holding briefly. Her eyes, framed with long dark lashes, were so deep a brown that they were almost black in the shaded light. At that moment, still without being pretty, she was almost beautiful, he thought.

And vulnerable, he thought next; separated from her husband for well over a year, living alone yet not legally free, not in a position to think of remarriage. Or did she already have her second husband lined up and if not, at least someone who was discreetly sharing her bed?

An interesting question. He dismissed it for the moment, picking up the menu. "What shall we have to eat?" he asked.

Rachel picked up hers with a surge of gratitude that he was dropping the matter of her marital situation.

That was how she wanted it. Some things were best let alone.

CHAPTER FOUR

Rachel had half forgotten the girl by the time she called her again. It was a Friday night this time, ten days after her first call.

"Oh, Martha," she said when Rachel answered the phone not long after her shift began. "It's me—remember?"

"Yes, of course," Rachel replied placing the light child-like voice.

"I tried to call you last night while my husband was down-town but I got someone named Linda." She made it sound a little reproachful that Rachel hadn't been available when she wanted to talk to her.

"We're on different nights." Rachel kept her tone non-committal with thoughts of the orientation program she had taken in which it was stressed that dependency on one particular aide should never be encouraged.

"Then Tuesdays and Fridays are your nights. Like my husband's teaching schedule. You're all volunteers, aren't you?"

"Yes. There's always one of us here so that if something comes up that you need help with any of the aides will be glad to give it."

But this statement made no impression on the girl; she hadn't taken the orientation program. "I'd rather talk to you, Martha," she said. "That's one of my problems. I get to lean on one particular person very easily. My husband, for instance—I lean on him too much, my shrink says."

Oh Lord, thought Rachel. Her shrink.

The girl continued confidingly, "There's no prowler tonight—or if there is, I haven't seen him. But I'm here all by myself and I thought I'd just say hi to you. So—Hi, Martha."

"Hi," said Rachel. It wouldn't hurt to let this lonely girl talk for another minute or two. Then she would remind her that someone else might be trying to get the line.

"Hey, you're nice," the girl said brightly. As if reading Rachel's mind, she added, "I know I mustn't take up too much of your time in case somebody needs to get Hot Line. But I, well—" The brightness went out of her voice. "It's always too quiet when I'm here alone and tonight I thought I'd tell you I wasn't really fair to my husband last week when I said I didn't think he'd take the prowler very seriously. He did, though. He wanted us to get a dog right away. He said it would be company and protection for me since he has to be out two nights a week."

"That sounds like a good idea," Rachel inserted.

"Maybe, but I said no. Because my cat Brindle would hate it. He's ten years old now—I've had him since I was thirteen—and it wouldn't be fair to him."

So she was twenty-three, older than Rachel had thought.

"Then he said maybe we could get someone to stay with me. Imagine that! Like having a baby-sitter. Like—" The girl's voice broke suddenly between laughter and tears.

"Do you like dogs?" Rachel asked, giving her a moment to collect herself.

"Oh yes. I had an Irish setter when I was a kid. I loved it so much I didn't want another dog after it got killed over in the Blue Ridge Mountains one fall. Someone shot it by mistake thinking it was a deer."

"Oh, what a shame," Rachel said. "I can imagine how you felt."

"It was awful. I thought it was the worst thing that could ever happen to me. It wasn't, of course. The worst thing of all was my mother's death. Nothing could ever be as awful as that." The girl gave a deep sigh and then asked, "Would it be all right if I told you about it? Just generally so that it wouldn't take too long?"

Was it good or bad for her to dwell on it? While Rachel hesitated over her reply the girl said, "My shrink tells me to talk about it all I want and maybe some day I'll get it all out of my system."

"Well then . . ." Rachel realized as she spoke that she was no longer inclined to doubt the girl's story about her mother's death. Her psychiatrist's advice, repeated so matter-of-factly, had the ring of truth in it.

"The night it happened my mother was alone in the house. We didn't have a live-in maid. It was October but it had been warm that day and the French door in the living room wasn't locked because we'd been going in and out.

"It wasn't long before Paul and I were to be married and a friend was giving a party for us that night . . ."

Paul. It was her first mention of her husband's name.

"My mother had been awfully busy that day and said she was going to bed early for once. She came upstairs with a book while I was getting dressed for the party. My step-father had already left for some meeting or other . . ."

The girl paused. "I don't think I've told you that my father died when I was eight and my mother remarried when I was twelve."

"No, you hadn't told me that." A difficult age to acquire a stepfather, Rachel thought. If she'd been a little younger it would probably have been easier for her.

And, from what she said next, for her mother too.

"I didn't want her to marry again," she said. "I was an only child, you see, and we were always very close, especially after my father died. I—well, I guess I resented Frank from the start. One thing I made a big issue of was that he was years younger than she, only thirty when they were married while she was nearly thirty-seven. She didn't look it, though. She was very beautiful with lots of men falling for her. Did I mention that before?"

"No."

"I'm not. Not even very pretty. I'm the image of my father, people say. But my mother was one of the most beautiful women you'd ever want to see."

The girl's voice had dropped to a monotone through repetition of what she must have told many times before. "The thing that made her maddest was for me to say he was marrying her for her money. It wasn't true, I know that now, looking back. He really was crazy about her right from the start. I wouldn't admit it at the time, though, and we had terrible scenes over him. But she went ahead and married him anyway and he came to live at our house . . .

"It was very bad the first few years until I went off to boarding school and then to college. My sophomore year in college I met my husband and after that I didn't mind quite so much about Frank."

But in the meantime, Rachel thought, she had probably made life hell for her mother and stepfather.

"She was killed only two weeks before the date set for my wedding," the girl continued. "We had the nicest talk upstairs that night. My mother got out some of her jewelry for me to pick out what I would like to have. There was this pendant that belonged to my father's grandmother, a lovely old piece, quite valuable, set with a star ruby and diamonds. My mother said I was to have it when I got married because it came from my father's side of the family. I tried it on and some of the other pieces and she left them on her bureau to put away later. The doorbell rang just then—it was Paul coming to pick me up—and she told me to be sure and lock the French door before I left. I said I would and kissed her good night"—anguish broke through the girl's monotone—"and went downstairs to let Paul in. Then the phone rang—a friend wanting to know if my cousin from Alexandria was coming to the party—and after I said yes we talked a bit. I thought I'd told Paul to lock the French door while I was on the phone but he said afterward that I hadn't. So it really was my fault, you see, that the prowler got in that way."

"Isn't it possible, though, that your mother went downstairs and checked it after you left?" Rachel suggested.

"Oh no. It was even partly open, my stepfather said, when he got home around quarter of eleven that night. My mother was lying dead on the hall floor upstairs with her head crushed in and—and blood everywhere.

"My stepfather called Paul at the party saying there'd been an accident and he and I and my cousin rushed home. And there she was—"

"How awful for you," Rachel said. "How awful."

"I nearly died of it. I—" the girl's voice broke. "I haven't got over it yet, my carelessness leaving the door unlocked and my mother dying like that." She drew in a ragged breath. "And over a few pieces of jewelry."

"They were all taken?"

"Yes."

"Was the prowler ever caught?"

"No. Not a trace of him or of the jewelry." The girl began to cry. "I don't think I ever will get over it. I almost had a nervous breakdown. That's when I started going to my first shrink."

There'd been more than one. The poor girl.

"We canceled our wedding plans, of course. I never wore the lovely dress I'd had made. We just got married quietly the week before Christmas. At first I didn't even want to move into this house that was all built and ready for us. I felt I couldn't bear it because my mother was so involved in all the plans for it from the start. But Paul said it would be rejecting everything she had done if we didn't live in it. So I said I would but I've never really been happy here. I don't know if I'd be happy anywhere."

"You've gone through a terrible time," Rachel said gently. "I'm so sorry."

"Thank you. And for letting me talk to you about it too."

The girl added through her tears, "I should hang up now, shouldn't I, in case someone's waiting for the line?"

"Yes, I'm afraid you should."

"Well then, good night, Martha. And thanks again for listening."

"You're welcome. Good night."

Shaken by the story as she made out a daily sheet on the call, Rachel hesitated over what category to put it in. None seemed right to her. Finally she wrote "Loneliness" in the space for remarks.

Poor girl, she thought. Poor human race.

The phone rang. She picked it up. "Hot Line, this is Martha. Can I help you?"

Still thinking about the girl as she drove home that night, it occurred to her that it would be easier than ever now to look up the mother's death. October three years ago and probably a front-page story. It seemed to Rachel that she ought to have some faint recollection of it herself.

Not necessarily, she realized, getting out of her car in the apartment house parking lot. She and Neil had taken a two-week trip to Greece in October three years ago and had a wonderful time.

Her phone started ringing as she unlocked her door. Her heart leaped wtih sudden fear. An accident, she thought, someone in her family.

But it was her husband calling from Florida. There was some hesitancy in his speech but he wasn't drunk as he had been the last time he called. Instead, he was belligerent.

"Where have you been till this hour?" he began. "I've been calling you since ten o'clock."

"Out," she made brief reply.

"Oh. Meaning it's none of my business?"

"Well . . ." She let her voice trail off into silence.

His tone changed immediately from accusation to pleading. "I miss you terribly tonight, Rachel. I keep thinking of all that we used to have together. Sometimes I can't believe it's over, can't stand the way things are between us now."

But he hadn't valued what they had at the time, Rachel thought. It was no use, though, putting the thought into words. It never would be.

She changed the subject asking, "How's your job going?"

"So-so. Everything's pretty dead here this winter." He was working for a maternal uncle who was in the real estate business.

"That's what your father said. I had dinner with him not long ago."

They talked a little about his father. Then Neil Carey said abruptly, "Are you sure, Rachel, absolutely sure, that you really want this divorce? I've never wanted it myself, you know."

That wasn't true, had not been true since months before their separation. But at the moment he believed it was true and she let it go unchallenged.

He went on to cite his grievances against her, alternating them with renewed pleadings that she reconsider her decision.

She listened mostly in silence and got him off the line as soon as she could.

But his call had worsened the low mood she was already in.

A drink might help.

She made one, took it out on her balcony and stood there while she drank it, drawing in deep breaths of the crisp night air and wishing that vainest of all wishes, that everything could be different. If only it could, she thought, if only . . .

"That's enough now, Luke, cut it out," she said firmly, breaking away from him at her door that Saturday night.

"Rachel—"

"No."

It took him a moment to quiet his breathing. Then, as

she unlocked the door, he asked, "Aren't you at least going to ask me in for a nightcap?"

"No. It's past one o'clock and you still have to drive back to Alexandria."

"Not really," he said recognizing defeat but still going through the motions. "There's no one waiting up for me in my apartment. No one to care," he made his tone plaintive, "if I ever get home."

Rachel laughed but wouldn't be drawn. "Thanks a lot for a nice evening," she said. "I enjoyed it very much."

He gave up then settling for a quick kiss that had no more than a trace of the demanding ardor he had shown earlier when she had found it difficult to fend him off.

"Good night, Rachel," he said. "Call you next week."

"Fine." She stood in the doorway until his long strides took him out of sight on the stairway, the door below closing behind him with a pneumatic hiss.

It was too bad if he was going to keep on making real passes, she thought, going inside and slipping the chain on the door. Because she wasn't ready, not nearly ready for them yet. All she wanted from him right now was his company, doing things together like going to a dinner theater tonight.

Luke Welford, getting into his car out in front, knew he had forced the pace a little more than he should have with Rachel. He really would have to take his time with her; she wasn't going to be an easy conquest.

But that was all right with him. More challenge to it. And at the moment there was no other girl of any great importance in his life.

The trouble with most of them was, they wanted to get serious right away. Which didn't suit him at all.

CHAPTER FIVE

The following Tuesday night, Mrs. Fuller, an older woman who had the shift ahead of Rachel's, told her when she arrived, "Some girl called just a few minutes ago asking for Martha. Caught on, you see, to when your shift is."

"Oh," said Rachel.

"Wanted to know if you'd be here at all tonight," Mrs. Fuller continued getting her coat off the rack. "I discouraged her all I could, saying I wasn't sure who was scheduled after me. Asked if there was any help I could give her. She said not."

"Oh," Rachel said again feeling guilty over the spark of interest the girl's call aroused in her. Where was the objective attitude she was supposed to take?

The trouble with it was that it didn't allow room for normal response.

Rachel turned the conversation away from the girl asking, "Have you been kept busy, Mrs. Fuller?"

"About as usual," filing her daily sheets. "No calls out of the ordinary, though. Well," closing the drawer, picking up her pocketbook, "I'll run along now. Good night, Rachel."

"Good night."

After Mrs. Fuller's departure Rachel checked the front and back doors to make sure they were double-locked, a procedure she didn't always remember to follow. Compensating for guilt pangs? she asked herself wryly.

Probably. What of it?

The phone rang as she sat down at the desk. The girl?

She picked it up, said, "Hot Line, this is Martha. Can I help you?" and wrote down the time, 8:05.

It wasn't the girl. It was an older woman, voice hesitant as so many of the voices were, saying, "I hope you can because I've got a very serious problem, miss."

"Yes?"

"It's about my daughter. I'm real upset about it and my husband, when he hears, will be even worse upset than I am."

Drugs or pregnancy?

Pregnancy, it turned out to be, after more beating about the bush from the woman.

"Two months pregnant close as we can figure it," the woman said. "And she's only fifteen, a sophomore in high school."

"Has your family doctor verified it?"

"No, we haven't been near him. I'd die of embarrassment. Him and his wife belong to our church, you see, and we know them pretty well. He's taken care of my daughter since she was a little thing. He'd be shocked to death, her getting herself in a fix like that."

"I don't think so," Rachel said. "Doctors get to be quite shockproof, you know."

"Still, I wouldn't for the world go to him." The woman's tone dismissed the prospect. "Abortion is what I want."

"I see." Feeling her way, Rachel asked, "Is that what your daughter wants too?"

"Yes indeed. She just wants to get rid of it and go on like nothing happened."

"Well then . . ." Rachel thought for a moment. "There are two ways to handle it," she said. "An out-of-town clinic or a gynecologist here in Monmouth. Of course, he might or might not be willing to perform the abortion. It would be his decision."

"If he'd do it, he'd put my daughter here in the Monmouth Hospital, wouldn't he?"

"Yes."

"I wouldn't have that. It would leak out. What about places in D.C.? Seems to me I've read about them."

Rachel flipped the file around to pregnancy where abortion was cross-indexed and gave the woman the names and addresses of two Washington clinics.

The woman thanked her and hung up.

At twenty minutes of ten the girl called and said in a frightened voice, "Oh Martha, the prowler's back. I saw him when I called Brindle in. And just now he rang the doorbell again."

"Have you called the police?"

"No. What if it was like the last time when they couldn't find him?"

"They'd still scare him off as they did before."

"I'd feel funny, though, if they couldn't find him."

"No reason you should. It's all in the night's work to them."

The girl finally said she would.

A little after ten-thirty she called back. "Same story as last time, Martha," she said. "Even the same cop who came before. He had just finished looking around the yard when my husband drove in. They're still out there so I mustn't talk too long. They're probably saying I imagined the whole thing."

"I doubt that," Rachel put in.

"I really didn't, Martha," the girl went on hurriedly. "There was someone out there and he rang the doorbell and then watched me peering out to see who it was. It's so mean. I can't understand why anyone should want to frighten me this way. Oh, the cop's leaving. I'd better hang up before my husband comes in. He's at the door now. Good night, Martha."

"Good night," Rachel said the girl's receiver clicking in the middle of it.

Three calls followed in quick succession. Making referrals, filling out daily sheets, she had no time to think about the girl until a lull set in and she could sit back in her chair with a cup of coffee.

Was the girl putting on an act, a good one, or was there really a prowler?

The first time she called she had asked if any sort of record was made of the call. Not a question usually asked. Building up support for her story, perhaps? The police would have a record, too, of her calls to them. Could the whole thing be intended to get her husband to stop teaching nights?

No amount of thought supplied an answer to any of these questions. The only thing Rachel felt sure of was the story about the mother's death. That tragedy, told in detail, had rung true from beginning to end.

If the rest was true, if there was a prowler both times, it didn't seem that he was actually trying to get into the house —not so far, at least—but just to frighten her, so why couldn't it be some neighborhood boy? Living nearby, he would see that the husband's car was gone and know that the girl was alone.

There were boys who would get their kicks out of something like that.

The police would think of that too, wouldn't they?

The phone interrupted Rachel's thoughts.

It was a wife in tears over marital problems. "My husband and I fight all the time," she began. "He just walked out on me now, slammed the door in my face when I ran after him and yelled that he was going to sleep over at his brother's. I—I—what did you say your name was, miss?"

"Martha."

"I can't begin to tell you what it's like, Martha. We fight over some of the craziest things. Tonight it started at supper over clam chowder. He said he liked it so I bought some. But how was I to know what kind he meant? I bought Manhattan and it turns out he only likes New England style. He said Manhattan wasn't real clam chowder, any stupid jerk knew that. And I said, 'Don't you call me a stupid jerk,' and then one word led to another, throwing things up at each other, and it's been going on for hours."

"How long have you been married?" Rachel was already looking up marriage in the file and finding the cross reference to marriage counselors.

"Ten months. But it don't look," the wife cried harder, "like we're going to make it to our first anniversary."

"Have you ever thought of getting help?"

"What kind of help?"

"A marriage counselor." Rachel had to explain their function. The wife had never heard of them.

"Are there some here in Monmouth?" she asked.

"Three. Would you like to have their names, their addresses and phone numbers?"

"I reckon so. I'm ready to try anything myself, the way my husband and I are fighting. I don't know what he'll say, though. Do they cost much?"

"I understand one of them is on a flat fee and that the other two have a sliding scale based on ability to pay. They would have to give you more details on that themselves, of course."

The wife took down the information and sounded a little calmer when she hung up.

There were no calls after that. In the quiet of the office as Rachel's shift neared its end her thoughts reverted again to the girl and her growing dependency on Rachel.

Tomorrow night she was due to attend the monthly session of the on-going training program where any problems the aides encountered were discussed.

If Rachel mentioned the girl's calls, Dr. Wright, the psychiatrist in charge of the program, would recommend that she do everything she could to discourage them, making it clear to the girl that Hot Line was not a counseling service.

Very sound recommendations. But since she already

knew what they would be, there seemed little point in bringing up the matter at all.

She had been working as a Hot Line aide for eight months now; she should be capable of handling it herself.

The trouble was, she had become interested in the girl in what was almost, in spite of only a few years' difference in their ages, a maternal sort of way.

Wasn't she lonely and neurotic enough herself right now without that?

Kindred spirits, she and the girl, it seemed.

Luke Welford called her the next morning and told her a friend of his was giving a party Friday night and that he would like to take her to it. "It's a bring-your-own-date party," he explained. "Civilized. No pot, no couples retreating to the bedroom. Got a nice big apartment too. Lives at the Risley Towers, if you know where it is."

"Yes, I do." Rachel conjured up an image of the vast soaring structure, one of the many that crowded the skyline off 95 on the way into Washington. Rabbit warrens she and Celia had called them in total rejection when they were apartment hunting themselves. The Risley Towers, in any case, had been beyond their means.

"He's a real good guy, works for the Labor Department. You'd like his friends. I know quite a few of them."

Friday night, though, Rachel would be covering Hot Line.

"It sounds great, Luke, but I'm afraid I can't make it," she said. "I already have plans for the evening."

"Come on now, Rachel, we both know plans can be changed," he protested, thinking as he spoke that this was the second time she had turned him down. Third time, actually, if he counted dinner with her father-in-law. He wasn't used to being turned down, didn't like it.

"Can't you say something urgent's come up," he suggested. "I really want to take you to this party."

"Well . . ." Rachel hesitated. She could call the chairman

and ask her to find someone to swap shifts with. It was through just such a swap that she had met Luke in the first place.

He caught the hesitancy in her voice. "Try to work it out," he said. "I'll call you this evening and you can let me know then."

"All right . . . Around seven?" she added thinking of the training program she was to attend that night. "I'll know by then."

She would like to go, she thought, dialing the chairman's phone number. No reason she shouldn't drive up to Alexandria in the late afternoon and spend the night at Celia and Bob's as she sometimes did when she had plans that took her into the Washington area. She could take them out to dinner somewhere before the party—it wouldn't begin much before nine o'clock—and have Luke pick her up at their apartment.

Wear her new silk pant suit or the coral dress Celia said was one of the most becoming things she had ever owned?

Rachel had committed herself to the party by the time the chairman of volunteers answered her phone.

Luke was pleased when he called Rachel that night; pleased that she was going to the party with him—she would do him credit in her well-bred understated way—and that she had changed her plans for him and was even arranging to stay in Alexandria overnight so that he wouldn't have to drive her back to Monmouth in the small hours of the morning.

He was gaining some ground with Rachel Carey, he reflected complacently.

But when he hung up after talking with her he felt less complacent. What other guy—or guys, for that matter—did she have on the string that she sometimes had other plans with? Even tonight, for example, she was getting ready to go out when he called her. No reason, of course, that there shouldn't be plenty of other guys who found her as attractive as he did. . . .

CHAPTER SIX

"Well, did you have a good time last night?" Celia asked looking up from the Washington *Post* when Rachel appeared in the living room doorway at a little after ten Saturday morning.

"Marvelous. Don't know when I've been to such a good party. All the right ingredients, bright people, a mixture of career types and young marrieds, lots of good talk, good food and drink. I enjoyed every minute of it. But Lord, I'm dead." Rachel yawned running her fingers through her short hair so that it stood on end. "Didn't get home until nearly three. Maybe a shower will help."

As she turned to go down the hall to the bathroom, Celia put the paper aside and said, "I'll make some fresh coffee while you're taking it. What would you like for breakfast?"

"Breakfast?" Rachel glanced back at her and made a face. "All I want is a large glass of juice and coffee. Got a bit of a hangover. Too many drinks at the party on top of the two we had at dinner. Where's Bob?"

"Out looking for gas. Station over on Duke Street's supposed to have some."

"We do better in Monmouth. Nobody pulls guns or starts fist fights in the gas station lines."

"Better manners, you mean, than people around here?"

"Maybe. Or," Rachel gave her an impish grin, "it might be because there aren't any lines. We just go and get gas."

"Oh, you!" Celia said and vanished into the kitchen.

She had coffee and a large glass of orange juice ready by the time Rachel emerged from the shower looking more wide awake.

"Just what I needed," she said gulping down the juice. "What'd you think of Luke?"

"He's certainly good-looking," said Celia.

Rachel eyed her aware of the ambivalence in her reply. "Yes, he is," she said sitting down at the table and stirring sugar into her coffee. "But you didn't like him."

"Heaven's sake, I didn't say that," Celia protested. "I barely met the man. Not long enough to form any real impression."

"But you formed one just the same. You didn't like him."

Celia sat down at the table. Her eyes, not quite as dark and brilliant as Rachel's, rested on her sister thoughtfully. "Well, as long as you insist on a snap judgment, I felt Luke Welford seemed a little too sure of himself. After all, he was meeting Bob and me, your family, for the first time and a touch of diffidence wouldn't have been out of place."

"But, Celia—"

"You asked so I'm telling you. He's what I call a smooth operator. Maybe some of it's his job. Working for an advertising agency, maybe he's used to selling himself along with his product. Or maybe the fact that he went into that kind of work makes it a question of which came first, the chicken or the egg. Anyway, Rachel, watch your step with him. With his looks and all that charisma he can take his pick, especially around here where eligible men are in short supply." Celia's tone softened. "It's just that you're pretty vulnerable right now, Rachel, and I don't want you to get hurt."

Rachel, drinking her coffee, looked at her sister and said dryly, "Always go to someone in your family if you want home truths."

"Nobody ever does want them," Celia retorted. "Oh well . . . More coffee?"

"Please." Rachel held out her cup and began talking about the party, the people she had met, but inwardly she was assessing Celia's comments on Luke Welford and the warning conveyed.

Her sister was right, of course. Rachel knew she was particularly vulnerable right now to Luke or, for that matter, to any man as attractive as he was. Last night, for instance, feeling her drinks, feeling gay and relaxed after a pleasant evening, she had responded too warmly to Luke's good night kisses, had permitted a few intimacies . . .

From now on she would draw back, keep him at a distance.

When he called a little later suggesting they have lunch together before her return to Monmouth Rachel said she couldn't, that she was getting ready to go home now.

"What's the hurry?" he asked.

"I have a dentist appointment." The lie came out convincingly.

They left it that he would call her sometime next week.

Tuesday night the girl was back on Hot Line.

"Hello, Martha," she said. "I hope you appreciate it that I didn't call you Friday night when the prowler paid me another visit. I just went right ahead on my own and called the police."

"Good for you. I wasn't here anyway." Trying to make a small break in the chain of dependency, she added, "We do change around, you know."

"You're mostly there Tuesdays and Fridays, though, aren't you?"

"Well . . . yes. But you haven't forgotten, have you, that I said any of the other aides would help you if they could?"

"I'd rather talk to you."

So what would Dr. Wright say to that?

"My stepfather was here Sunday and he and Paul were talking about the prowler," the girl continued. "They feel, the doorbell being rung and all, that it's probably some neighborhood kid."

"I've thought of that myself," Rachel said.

"Have you? The cop brought it up, too, the other night when he came. If it is, I think I know which one. A high school kid from down the street getting back at me because we had an argument not long before the prowler came here for the first time. I caught the kid throwing stones at Brindle. Poor cat ran all the way up a tree, scared to death. If he's the one, I'm going to figure out some way to prove it; set some sort of a trap for him."

"But—what if it's someone else?"

"Oh, I'll be careful. But the more I think about it, the more I'm sure it's that kid. And I've had all I'm going to take from him. He improved on his routine the other night, by the way. Not only rang the doorbell but rapped on a window too. And as usual, had vanished by the time the police arrived. At least it was a different cop; the one who came the other times was off duty."

"Did he say anything except that it might be a kid?"

"No, he just looked around and didn't have much of anything to say. They must be sick of my calls. I'm not going to call them again. I'm not so frightened now that I feel pretty sure it's that kid. I'll handle it myself next time he shows up."

This complete turnabout from fear to self-confidence seemed extreme to Rachel. "Have you given any thought to having a talk with the boy and his parents?" she asked. "Or having the police go to them?"

"They won't do it. I mentioned it Friday night and the cop said they couldn't just barge in without some sort of evidence against him."

"But you and your husband could."

"Oh, I don't know, Martha. I haven't even suggested it to Paul. The way he's been acting, it's as if he doesn't believe me half the time; thinks I'm either exaggerating or making the whole thing up; that it's all tied in with my not wanting him to teach at night."

Rachel said nothing aware of how often she had shared the husband's viewpoint.

Bitterness came into the girl's voice as she continued, "He's fed up with it. Fed up with me too. Everyone is. My shrink says I shouldn't take such a negative attitude toward people but how can I help it? I know how they feel. My stepfather, for one, couldn't care less what happens to me. That doesn't matter, it's partly my fault anyway. But my cousin in Alexandria, the one who was there the night my mother died, really hurts. We were so close growing up but I never see him nowadays. I felt so lonely one night a little while ago that I called him up and told him about the prowler and how upset I was. All he said was not to worry about it too much. I could tell from the way he spoke that he thought I was imagining a lot of it. I hoped he would offer to come down but he didn't. So that's how much he cares what happens to me."

Or how little he believed in the prowler, Rachel thought while she said consolingly, "Maybe he's too busy to come right now."

"Not that busy. Oh well, there's not much you can do about it, is there, Martha?" The girl, trying to sound jaunty, burst into tears and hung up.

"Lord," Rachel said aloud, half exasperated, half distressed.

The phone rang just as she finished making out a daily sheet on the call. She picked it up. "Hot Line, this is Martha. Can I help you?"

"If you don't mind talking to me for a few minutes it might help a little," the woman on the line said. "That's all anyone can do for me. Because I've had it."

"I'm sorry you feel like that."

"Well, I do. I've had all I can take from that two-timing bastard I married thirty years ago. I'm at the end of my rope."

"You mean you're going to leave him?" Rachel asked tentatively.

"Oh, I'm going to leave him all right. Forever and ever."

There was a slight thickness in the woman's voice. Had she been drinking?

"He's just got himself a new girl friend. One too many, Martha—isn't that what you said your name was?"

"Yes."

"I told him that when he went out tonight. One too many, I said. He didn't answer, didn't even bother to make up an excuse. He never does any more, just comes and goes as he pleases. He'll be freer than ever after tonight."

"You're—walking out on him?"

"All the way, Martha. I cried for an hour when he left but what good did that do? I went out in the kitchen and started to do the dinner dishes and then, all of a sudden, I thought, Why bother? So I got out the sleeping pills and took them all, every single one."

"Oh no . . ."

The woman laughed wildly. "Double surprise for the bastard when he gets home. Dirty dishes in the sink and me dead here on our bed. Let him do the dishes. Let him explain why I committed suicide. Everyone knows what a womanizer he is."

This was the crisis situation Rachel had hoped she would never have to face.

"Are you sure you want to go through with it?" she asked, trying to keep her voice steady as emergency procedures discussed during her training program raced through her mind. "This gift of life—"

"Some gift," the woman cut in. "I got short-changed."

"But still— Oh, one moment please, my other phone's ringing. If you'll just hang on I'll get right back to you."

"All right."

Rachel snatched up the unlisted phone and carried it on

its long cord into the kitchen to make sure the woman wouldn't hear her dialing the police emergency number.

It was answered immediately. "Police Department, Officer Caldwell."

"This is Hot Line, Officer, Rachel Carey speaking. I have a woman on the phone who says she's taken an overdose of sleeping pills. Will you notify the telephone company while I try to keep her talking long enough for them to trace the call?"

"Right away."

Rachel ran back to the desk almost afraid to pick up the Hot Line phone for fear the woman had hung up.

But she said, "Hi, Martha, I'm still here."

Rachel could hardly understand her, though, her speech had thickened so much.

"It's kind of lonely lying here all by myself waiting—to die." The woman was making an effort to articulate each word. "No one—I could call—except you. Because—they'd try to—stop me."

Rachel felt a pang of guilt. She was trying to stop the woman herself, had lied to her, tricked her, it might even be said. Actually, though, wasn't her call to Hot Line a cry for help whether she realized it or not?

But this wasn't the moment to explore ethical considerations, the woman's right to take her own life if she wanted to.

Instead, keep her talking.

"Do you have any children?" Rachel asked.

"Two. But they're grown up—married. Own—lives—to live."

"You're their mother, though, and even if they are married they still need you in lots of ways."

The woman mumbled something Rachel didn't catch and then, trying again, said, "Nobody—needs me. Least of all—my hus—"

The phone dropped with a thud from her hand.

"Ma'am?" Rachel said urgently. "Are you still there?"

A far-off sigh was the only answer.

"Ma'am?"

There was no answer at all.

But the woman hadn't hung up, the line was still open.

How long did it take to trace a call and who had the authority to do it?

Rachel couldn't remember what had been said about it during orientation program; what stood out in her mind was the emphasis placed on keeping them talking as long as possible.

She sat with the receiver pressed so hard against her ear that it had a painful red ridge around it she discovered when the crisis was over.

No sound came from the other end of the line but it was still open.

Rachel had no idea how much time passed before she reached for the other phone and dialed the police again. The same officer answered.

"This is Hot Line," she said. "Has the phone company been able to trace that call yet?"

"Yes, ma'am. They gave me the address a couple of minutes ago and I just hung up now from calling the Rescue Squad. You did real well keeping that woman talking."

"She wasn't talking. She's been unconscious most of the time since I called you. I heard the phone drop."

"Well, the Rescue Squad's on their way by now. They'll take care of it, break the door down if they have to."

"I hope it's not too late."

"They'll do all they can, ma'am, just like you did all you could."

"Well, thank you," Rachel replied. "But you had a part in it too."

"All in the night's work, ma'am," he said cheerfully, and hung up.

Rachel hung up herself but still left the Hot Line phone off the hook. She needed a moment or two to collect herself before she had to answer any sort of inquiry.

She sank back in the chair sighing with relief that she had handled the situation adequately. Even an older, more experienced aide like Mrs. Fuller couldn't have done anything more than she had done herself.

Presently she hung up the Hot Line phone and reached for the pad. The woman had called at nine-forty. It was now five minutes past ten. Only twenty-five minutes had passed since the drama of life or death began.

An unwanted life—or was it really?—would be restored if the Rescue Squad reached that poor desperate woman in time.

The phone rang, an obscene call.

"It's pathetic that you can't find anything better to do with yourself than pester people this way," she said sharply, and hung up.

Driving home that night her thoughts were still centered on the woman. For the moment she had lost sight of her earlier call from the girl.

CHAPTER SEVEN

There were no calls from her for over two weeks. By Friday of the second week Rachel, at odd intervals, wondered if she would ever hear from her again or if the girl had decided she could handle her problems by herself.

But that Friday night the girl called. Without the preliminaries of a greeting she said, "I think I just made a perfect fool of myself, Martha."

"Oh." Rachel put down the time, 9:50, on a daily sheet and asked, "How'd you do that?"

"Well, the prowler was here early tonight, about eight o'clock, ringing the doorbell, rapping on windows, the whole routine. It made me so mad I didn't even think about calling the police. I went right down the street to talk to that kid and his parents."

"Was he home?"

"Yes. He denied that he'd had anything to do with it and said he'd been upstairs in his room all evening doing his homework. His parents backed him up. But it's a big house, Martha, and I got a look at the layout. There's a family room added on in back where the parents were watching TV. It seemed to me that the kid is free to come and go as he pleases unless the parents check on him. Which they admitted they hadn't done tonight since he went upstairs at seven o'clock or so. He could have gone out any time at all tonight without their knowledge, you see."

"But you can't prove he was at your house," Rachel said.

"I know. But on the other hand, the boy can't prove he wasn't."

"Well, if he's the one, maybe you scared him off by going there. At least it seems as if his parents will keep a closer check on him."

"I hope so," the girl said. "Whether it's that kid or not, I've had about all I can take of it. I told Paul the last time it happened that if they won't change his schedule to just day classes he's going to have to look for a job somewhere else. There are other community colleges within driving distance."

One more fact revealed. The girl's husband taught at a community college. Prince William? It was the nearest one to Monmouth.

"What did he say?"

"That he didn't want to; that he likes it where he is. He brought up getting a dog again. Or else, he said, we could sell the house—and move into an apartment."

People and their problems, Rachel thought. Sometimes she got sick of them, most of all her own.

Like Luke, still making advances. She wasn't going to go to bed with him, had told him so flat out the other night when he brought her home. But she would miss his company, she knew, if he dropped her because she tried to keep him in his place.

What kind of a world was it, though, where a man, on relatively short acquaintance, felt aggrieved over something like that? Rachel's mother, strict in her views and bringing up her family the same way, would be shocked that Rachel actually weighed the advantages and disadvantages of the situation instead of telling Luke never to darken her door again. Her mother would probably be just as shocked that part of the problem was the response Luke sometimes aroused in her.

Sitting with the phone to her ear, not really listening to the girl at the moment, Rachel composed a statement for her mother's benefit. "After all, Ma," it ran, "I'm not an innocent young girl any more. I was a wife for four years and

Neil, sober, was a good lover and got me used to a man . . ."

A statement that would never be delivered to her strait-laced mother.

Rachel returned her attention to the girl, who was now talking about her cousin's neglect of her. "It hurts me so much," she was saying. "Our closeness in the past and the fact that he was there the night my mother died should have brought us together even more. But he practically ignores me nowadays."

The plaint had been made before. Rachel repeated her answer to it, that perhaps the cousin was just too busy. Then she added, "Also, there are people who avoid troubles. Perhaps your cousin is like that."

After a moment's silence the girl said, "Well, yes, Luke is, I guess. Fair-weather friend, fair-weather cousin."

Her cousin's name was Luke and he lived in Alexandria.

There could be two of them; Luke wasn't that uncommon a name. But two of them so familiar with Monmouth that they never had to ask directions from one place to another?

It didn't seem likely.

Rachel puzzled over it after the girl hung up. How odd, she thought, that if it was the same one he had never mentioned having a cousin in Monmouth.

Or was it? Maybe not. Maybe he was no longer interested enough in the girl to even mention her existence. After all she had problems, something Luke did try to avoid, never asking Rachel about hers, her impending divorce or much of anything that went beyond the moment.

That was Luke's life style. Also, it might be that he just thought his having a cousin in Monmouth was none of Rachel's business. Which it wasn't really.

But still . . .

She wouldn't be able to help thinking of it when Luke took her out to dinner tomorrow night.

She must ask him to dinner soon at her place . . .

The phone rang taking Rachel's mind off the whole matter. No use to dwell on it anyway. Not even knowing the girl's name, she couldn't mention it to Luke unless she was prepared to bring in Hot Line and the girl's calls to her. She wasn't, of course, so that was the end of it.

Except for the lingering thought that there was something a little callous about the way Luke ignored his cousin. When the mother was alive and there were parties and gaiety, he had been part of it all. But now when there was only a stubborn clinging to sorrow Luke had nothing to do with the girl.

Fair-weather friend, she had said. Fair-weather cousin.

What was her husband like? All Rachel really knew of him was that he stood on his own feet about keeping his job, not taking the prowler seriously enough, it seemed, to give it up. Did lack of concern for her welfare come into it?

What was the girl's stepfather like? Wicked stepfather, according to her. Not the right adjective. In fairy tales it was always a wicked stepmother. None that Rachel could recall at the moment had much to say about stepfathers.

Were there only kind stepfathers, neutral stepfathers, cipher stepfathers? Come to think of it, it was men who wrote the fairy tales about wicked stepmothers. Something Freudian there?

Rachel laughed at herself dismissing the matter.

Her next thought was that tonight at least the girl wasn't making up her story of a prowler, not when she had gone to the neighbor's house to challenge the son.

After that night there was another gap between the girl's calls. If her prowler was the kid down the street perhaps he had been scared off, Rachel thought, even though his non-appearance would be a giveaway in itself.

Tuesday of the second week that the girl hadn't called was a warm bright day, so pleasant that Rachel and a friend packed a picnic lunch and spent the afternoon at a park nearby. Forsythia was in full bloom along the roadsides, crocuses almost gone, redbud and gum trees bursting into bud, dandelions spangling green lawns with yellow.

Stretched out on a blanket in the park listening to a chorus of birds, Rachel felt that it was enough just to be alive on a day like this, aware of every scent and sight and sound. The thought crossed her mind that if all the troubled people who would call her on Hot Line tonight were here in the park this afternoon the problems of many of them would dwindle away and their calls would not be made.

Her own problems seemed small today.

But they came back with a jolt that evening when she drove into the parking lot in back of the Hot Line office. A Corvette was parked there along with two or three other cars, the overflow apparently from whatever was going on at the Lafayette Inn across the street. It was a blue Corvette. Neil's car, she thought for a heart-stopping moment. He was here somewhere waiting for her.

Reason reasserted itself. Neil knew nothing about her work at Hot Line and in any case was still in Florida. Just last night when she talked with her father-in-law on the phone he had mentioned a call from Neil on Sunday.

Even so, Rachel walked over for a closer look at the car and saw that it was brand new whereas Neil's was almost three years old.

Just a coincidence, she thought, walking down the driveway and around to the front door.

But it had shaken her a little. It was a reminder of the finality of the breakup of her marriage that just the sight of a car she thought was Neil's had brought a sense of shock and total rejection of him.

Mrs. Fuller greeted her with complaints about the state of the world, whose troubles she blamed on Watergate and in curious juxtaposition, it seemed to Rachel, the welfare state.

"Couldn't believe my ears," she snorted, "this woman calling to ask if Hot Line would go bail for her son who was arrested last night for stealing a car. I don't know what's going to come of it, people looking for handouts all the time. All this lawlessness in the White House makes it worse, sets a bad example."

"What did you tell the woman?" Rachel inquired interestedly.

"I said she'd have to talk to the police or the Commonwealth's attorney about it. We certainly don't have a referral on it here." Another snort. "Free bail as I live and breathe. What next?"

"If the son is a juvenile and it's a first offense, he might be released into the parents' custody without bail," Rachel commented.

"It's not a first offense. The woman said they released him that way the last time he stole a car. There's no harm in her son, she said. It's just that he loves cars and they can't afford one."

Mrs. Fuller, still snorting and shaking her head, finally said good night. Rachel opened her book and settled down to her shift.

The girl called a few minutes later. "Haven't talked to you in a long time, Martha," she said.

Her voice sounded different, Rachel thought. Too bright, too brittle.

"It's been a marvelous day, hasn't it?" the girl continued. "I spent most of it outside puttering around the yard. What did you do?"

"Went on a picnic."

"How nice."

They might have been any two friends chatting.

"My tulips and daffodils are way up. I have a handsome new daffodil, Martha. Its color is almost black. I'm watching over it like mad. Do you garden?"

"I used to but I'm living in an apartment right now."

"Oh. Well, I feel quite organized after all I've accomplished today. At the moment I'm going through some old family papers that I brought home from my mother's the other day. I'm nearly finished with them and then I'm going out."

"Out for the evening?"

"No, just outside to see if the prowler shows up. That kid, I mean. He showed up again Friday night for the first time since I went to his house. I know Paul thinks I make too much of it—when he believes me at all—and before I'm done I'm going to prove to him that it really has been going on all along."

"But you don't know—"

"That it's that kid? No, but I'm fairly sure of it. And tonight is a nice night to prowl and just as nice to wait outside to catch him. I've got a chair out there in a good dark spot and I'll give him half an hour or so. If someone else shows up, I'll keep out of sight and try to get a look at him."

"Did you tell your husband about doing this?"

"No. Why should I? He's not that interested."

"Oh but I'm sure he wouldn't want you to—"

"Good night, Martha," the girl interrupted. "If the prowler appears, maybe I'll call you back later and tell you about it."

She hung up before Rachel could say anything more.

Rachel felt uneasy over the call. The girl's bright brittle tone, almost defiant, was new as if she were setting out to do battle with the prowler. But the kind of man—or adolescent boy—who would frighten a woman alone in a house that way was not anyone to try to corner or identify. As twisted as he must be, there was no telling how he'd react.

It was all meant to show her husband that she could take care of herself, Rachel conjectured. Or to get back at him if they'd had a fight—which seemed probable from her tone—before he left for his classes.

The phone broke in on Rachel's thoughts. As soon as she hung up it rang again, a man with a long complicated story about his neighbor in the other half of their duplex house who played his TV until all hours.

After she got him off the phone with the suggestion that the police could tell him what the regulations were on how loud a TV could be played late at night another call came in.

It was almost nine o'clock before Rachel found time to get a glass of water in the kitchen. While she drank it she looked out the back window at the parking lot. The blue Corvette was gone. It seemed silly that this should give her a sense of relief but still it did.

The phone brought her back to the desk.

It turned out to be one of the busiest nights she had ever spent on Hot Line.

She was on her way home when it occurred to her that the girl hadn't called her back.

Apparently the prowler had not appeared.

CHAPTER EIGHT

Rachel had a one-day substitute teaching assignment scheduled for Wednesday and before she went to bed set her alarm for quarter past six.

But when it went off in the morning she told herself it wouldn't hurt to take ten more minutes and settled deeper under the covers. The next time she opened her eyes it was past seven o'clock.

In the rush to get dressed she had no thought of turning on the morning news, local or national.

She drove to Falls Church right after school to have dinner with a friend and didn't get home until ten o'clock that night, picking up the Monmouth *Register* at her door as she unlocked it.

She made herself a nightcap and sat down with the Monmouth paper and the Washington *Post,* not even looked at that morning.

She opened the Monmouth *Register* first to glance at the more recent headlines it had to offer. Watergate occupied the right-hand side of the front page but the left-hand headline took her attention away from it. "Local Woman Murdered," it said, and above in boldface type, "Prowler Suspected."

Prowler. Rachel caught her breath. She glanced at the accompanying picture of a young woman with the caption, "Slaying Victim," and went on to the story.

"The body of Mrs. Amy Gardner, 23," she read, "was discovered by her husband, Paul W. Gardner, in their Britton Road home.

"Gardner, returning at 10:45 P.M. from Prince William Community College where he conducts evening classes, found the body lying on the kitchen floor and immediately notified Monmouth police.

"Death, pending autopsy, apparently resulted from head wounds inflicted by a heavy instrument.

"Captain Samuel Betz, in charge of the investigation, disclosed today that Mrs. Gardner had called the police several times in the past two months to complain of a prowler. No trace of one was ever found by the responding officers but this possibility, he said, is being considered in the course of the investigation.

"Mrs. Gardner, daughter of the late Mrs. Stella Lambert (see story page 4) and the late Richard Lundy, was a native and lifelong resident of Monmouth. She was a graduate of Stuart Hall and attended Mary Baldwin College. Besides her husband, she is survived by her stepfather, Franklin D. Lambert of Monmouth."

The girl who had been calling her all these weeks. Rachel reached for her drink on the table beside her, so shaken that she had to use both hands to steady the glass as she picked it up.

The girl's name was Amy Gardner. She had regarded Rachel as a friend, had called her just last night and talked in that brittle defiant way about catching the prowler whose very existence Rachel had sometimes questioned.

But he did exist, it seemed, and had caught her instead.

The paper open on her lap, her glass still held in both hands, Rachel studied Amy Gardner's picture. She looked very young—her yearbook picture, perhaps, from Stuart Hall?—a girl of average looks with a wide trusting gaze and a wistful suggestion of a smile. Amy Gardner, not quite grown up at twenty-three, never now to grow up . . .

Just last night she had called . . .

Rachel finished her drink in a few quick gulps, and only then, still absorbing the shock, did she turn to page four.

There the headline read: "Tragic Mother-Daughter Coincidence."

The story on the mother's murder was much as Amy Gardner had told it to Rachel. The date was October 23, 1970, details of the robbery connected with it were included and mention made of the French door through which it was assumed the prowler had gained entrance to the house. As with the daughter, the mother's body had been found by her husband, Franklin D. Lambert, Monmouth City Planner, on his return from a meeting.

The prowler had never been apprehended nor any of the valuable jewelry recovered. Amy Gardner—Lundy then—prostrated with grief, had been placed under a doctor's care and her wedding to Paul Gardner, scheduled for early November and considered one of the social events of the season, had been postponed.

The concluding paragraph stated that Mrs. Lambert, noted for her beauty and social leadership, had been the widow of Richard Lundy, president of the Monmouth Savings and Loan Association, and had married Franklin Lambert eight years before her death.

Rachel laid aside the paper and got to her feet to wander distractedly around the room. The one fixed point in the turmoil of her thoughts was the realization that she would have to go to the police herself and tell them about her conversations with the dead girl.

But not tonight, not at—she glanced at her watch—twenty minutes of eleven.

She shivered at the thought that last night at this time Amy Gardner had been lying dead in her house all alone with a few more minutes to pass before her husband came home and found her.

Tomorrow morning, Rachel thought, she would go to the police. First of all, though, she would have to call Mrs. Holt, the executive director of the Mental Health Association, since the information she had to give involved Hot Line.

Rachel went to bed but it was two o'clock before she finally fell asleep.

It was still dark when she woke up, the illuminated hands on her bedside clock showing six-thirty, too early to get up but, with thoughts of Amy Gardner instantly flooding her mind, no prospect of going back to sleep.

Instead, she began reviewing once again their phone conversations, particularly the last one two nights ago. She fretted to herself that she hadn't given the girl an emphatic warning that might have stopped her from trying to trap the prowler. What if she had said to her, "Look, this plan of yours could be dangerous. Forget it."

But she hadn't been that forthright.

Maybe it wouldn't have made any difference, anyway, considering the mood Amy Gardner was in Tuesday night.

At seven o'clock, heavy-eyed from lack of sleep, Rachel got up, made coffee and brought in the Washington *Post*. The dead girl's picture, the same one that was in the Monmouth paper, looked out at her from the Metro section that covered suburban news.

The story was much the same, too, a shorter version that included only a brief paragraph on the similar manner of the mother's death.

Rachel had no appetite for breakfast but made herself eat a piece of toast, then took a shower and got dressed. At eight-thirty she called Mrs. Holt who should be leaving soon for her office downtown.

Mrs. Holt listened to Rachel's story. From the tone of her questions she wasn't too happy over Hot Line's involvement in a murder but at the end she said, "You're quite right, of course, the police should have this information. Now let's see . . . I have a conference scheduled for ten o'clock. Suppose I call and find out if anyone who's on the case can see us around nine. Is that all right with you, Rachel?"

"Oh yes. Whatever time suits you."

"I'll check on it and call you back."

Within minutes Mrs. Holt was back on the line. "Captain Betz will see us as soon as we get there. I'll meet you outside."

The older woman, living nearer, arrived first, waiting for Rachel in the parking lot that spread out on both sides of the new building occupied by the police department.

The desk man directed them along a corridor to Captain Betz's office, the last one on the right, a bright clean-looking room with modern metal furniture.

The captain stood up from his desk to greet them, a tall heavily built man in early middle age wearing a well-fitting uniform.

Mrs. Holt introduced herself and Rachel. When they were seated she took charge saying in her brisk competent way, "Before Mrs. Carey tells you her story, Captain, I'd like to ask that you try to keep Hot Line out of it as far as anything getting into the papers is concerned. I'm sure you can well imagine the calls there would be if Hot Line received any publicity on this."

Betz nodded. "Nut calls. Every kook in town on the phone. We've had a couple of them already. But if anything about Mrs. Carey's information has to come out, I can assure you that we'll do our best to keep it anonymous."

He tipped his swivel chair back and smiled at Rachel encouragingly. "Well, Mrs. Carey? Carey . . . Weren't you the one who covered that recent suicide attempt?"

"Yes." Rachel smiled back with relief. "I'm glad you said attempt, Captain. I watched the paper for a couple of days but there wasn't a death that might have been that woman's. I assumed she was all right but I'm glad to have it confirmed."

"You handled it just fine. I saw the report on it."

Rachel was pleased by the compliment and that it had been paid to her in front of Mrs. Holt who wasn't going to be at all pleased over how many conversations Rachel had

had with Amy Gardner that were not based on specific referrals or services.

The next moment the captain asked, "Would you mind if I taped your story, Mrs. Carey? Much simpler than having you repeat it all later in a formal statement."

"No, I don't mind," Rachel said.

He got up, pulled forward a tape recorder on a stand, started it and said, "All right, Mrs. Carey, just go ahead. Give your name and address first, please, and the background of your acquaintance with Mrs. Gardner."

Rachel nodded and began, "My name is Rachel Harrison Carey. I live at 389 Monroe Street, Monmouth, apartment 212 . . ."

She tried to keep the story in chronological order, beginning with Amy Gardner's first call in February and going on to the last one Tuesday night.

Betz made notes on a pad and when Rachel was finished consulted a file on his desk and said, "Tuesday, February 12 is the first record we have of a complaint about a prowler from Mrs. Gardner. That fits in with her first call to you, doesn't it?"

"Yes, that's about right," Rachel replied.

"I'd like to have a record of all her calls to you, Mrs. Carey, dates, times and so forth. Can you get it for me?"

"I'll start on it tomorrow night when I'm at the Hot Line office," Rachel said.

Betz moved on to the boy down the street. "According to our records she didn't know his name, she just knew where he lived. He shouldn't be too hard to locate, though . . . Would you say, Mrs. Carey, that she called you every time this prowler showed up?"

"Mostly but not always," Rachel said.

"You became quite friendly, didn't you? She seems to have told you a lot about her troubles, her mother's death, her fears over being left alone when her husband was teaching night classes."

"Yes, we did become quite friendly, Captain." Rachel slanted a glance at Mrs. Holt who wore a carefully noncommittal expression.

Betz's pale blue eyes were fastened on Rachel as he said, "With these talks going on for nearly two months, Mrs. Carey, you must have formed some impression of what kind of a person you were dealing with. What conclusions did you reach about her?"

Rachel hesitated, suddenly conscious of the tape recorder. But speaking nothing but good of the dead hardly applied in the present situation. "Well, not too mature or too stable," she began. "And a real mother fixation made worse by guilt because she'd left that door unlocked the night of her mother's death. . . ."

Rachel paused and then asked a question of her own. "Was anything stolen from the Gardners' the other night, Captain?"

"I've asked Mr. Gardner to check on that. If there was no robbery it won't prove anything, one way or the other. Whoever killed Mrs. Gardner could have been frightened off by something."

"What time was she killed?" Rachel asked. "The paper didn't say."

"The paper didn't know," Betz replied. "We won't really know ourselves until we get the autopsy report later today. But the medical examiner, who saw her around midnight, estimated the time of death as up to two to three hours earlier."

"Then it could have been as late as just before Mr. Gardner got home," Rachel commented. "If the murderer intended to steal anything, that could have frightened him off."

"Yes." Betz did not add that Paul Gardner's arrival home fell too closely within the estimated time of death to give him an alibi.

At this point Mrs. Holt looked at her watch. It was five

of ten, time for her to leave, she said, for her ten o'clock appointment.

"After all that Mrs. Carey's told you, Captain, do you still think you'll be able to keep Hot Line out of it?" she asked as he opened the door for her.

"We'll do our best, Mrs. Holt," he said.

He left the door open when he returned to his desk and took Rachel through her last conversation with Amy Gardner again.

It seemed to her that she was repeating it almost word for word until she was near the end. She hesitated then and said, "Now that I think of it, she mentioned something she was going to do before she went outside to watch for the prowler—or maybe it was something she had to finish first."

"Some household chore, you mean, like doing the dishes?"

"No, that wasn't it. But some small thing—" Rachel shook her head. "I can't recall what it was. But does it matter, a few minutes more or less before she went outside?"

"Probably not. She wasn't killed for another hour or so at least. But if you think of it, let me know, will you? Just for the record."

"Yes, I will."

Captain Betz thought for a moment and then said, "Well, I reckon that's it for now, Mrs. Carey. There may be points I'll want to go over with you again after the tapes are transcribed but meanwhile things seem pretty well covered. Someone will give you a call within the next couple of days on coming in to sign your statement. I certainly do appreciate—"

The telephone interrupted him. He was quick to pick it up, having given instructions that calls were to be held during his interview with Rachel unless something important developed.

"Yes?" he said, listened, said, "Zatso? Well, tell him I'll be with him in a minute. No, wait." He took time to consider the matter and then, glancing at Rachel, said, "On second thought, send him in now."

"Gardner's just arrived to report some of his wife's jewelry missing," he informed her. "You might as well meet him. He'll have to be told about his wife's Hot Line calls anyway. I'm sure you realize they can't remain completely confidential, Mrs. Carey."

"I guess not," Rachel said keeping to herself her further realization that the captain's sudden decision to have her meet Paul Gardner was made for the purpose of observing his reactions with Rachel present when he heard about his wife's Hot Line calls to her.

Which meant, she reflected, that Paul Gardner must be high on the list of suspects. At the head of it, no doubt. But wasn't that always the case with the husband?

Footsteps approached and a moment later Paul Gardner halted in the doorway.

"Come in, Mr. Gardner," Betz said, and then stood up to perform introductions with punctilious courtesy. "This is Mr. Gardner . . . Mrs. Carey."

"How do you do," Rachel said.

He murmured a response with a faintly puzzled look over her being there and handed a folded sheet of paper to Betz. "Here's the list of missing pieces, close as I can tell."

Rachel had a moment to study him as he turned to the captain. He was medium tall with light brown hair of medium length, a strand of it fallen across his forehead. He had a thin scholarly face dominated by dark-rimmed glasses and lines around the mouth that suggested good humor under normal circumstances. At the moment, though, it was taut with strain. There was nothing cold or overbearing about his manner or appearance as Rachel had thought there might be from her conversations with his wife.

It crossed her mind, as Betz looked at the list, that Amy Gardner must have been killed well before her husband got home for there to have been time enough to steal her jewelry.

Unless, she thought next, Paul Gardner had got rid of it himself to create just that impression.

But looking at him again as he sat down, Rachel suddenly hoped that someone else had killed his wife.

Captain Betz put the list aside saying, "I'll go over it with you in a few minutes, sir. Meanwhile, I mustn't take up any more of Mrs. Carey's time." He paused deliberately and then added, "Mrs. Carey has been giving me information connected with your wife's death, Mr. Gardner. She's a Hot Line volunteer. You've heard of them, haven't you?"

"Well, yes, an article in the paper now and then," Gardner replied. "But I'm afraid I don't understand just how Mrs. Carey—?"

Betz answered the question left hanging in midair. "She's on duty a couple of nights a week at the Hot Line office, Mr. Gardner," he said. "Your wife has been calling her off and on for the past two months."

Whatever hope the captain had of some sign of guilt, dismay, even alarm over this disclosure came to nothing. Bewilderment was the only expression Paul Gardner's face revealed as he looked at Rachel and said, "She called you, Mrs. Carey? But why? She never mentioned it to me—what did she—?"

If his reaction wasn't genuine he was a damn good actor, Betz thought sourly. Either way, confronting him with Rachel Carey had been a waste of time.

He left it to Rachel to reply. She explained the reason for Amy Gardner's calls as briefly as she could and then added, "It wasn't always the prowler, though, Mr. Gardner. Sometimes it was just loneliness, the need for someone to talk to."

A contrite look touched his face. "I'm afraid I didn't pay enough attention to her fears."

There was no profit for Betz in this exchange. "I won't

keep you any longer, Mrs. Carey," he said firmly getting to his feet. "Thank you very much for coming in."

"But—" Paul Gardner was slower to rise and looked a little frustrated. "I'd like to talk to you again sometime, Mrs. Carey, about Amy's calls—would you mind?"

"No, not at all."

Betz frowned. He didn't fancy further contact between Rachel and the husband, who was a close second to the prowler on his list of suspects. Not that anything she had told him could put her in danger from Gardner or anyone else but still, he didn't fancy it.

He thanked her again for coming in and hurried her to the door, standing there until she was out of sight.

He went back to his desk then and picked up the list of missing jewelry.

"Now let's see, Mr. Gardner," he said.

CHAPTER NINE

As Rachel went down the front steps of the police station a coffee shop directly opposite was a reminder of how sketchy her breakfast had been.

She crossed the street and went in. There were few other patrons at that in-between time of the morning. Seated in a booth near the front, her order of a poached egg on toast and coffee was soon served.

Before she was finished the door opened and Paul Gardner came in. They saw each other at the same moment. He walked over to her and asked, "May I join you, Mrs. Carey?"

"Yes, do."

He sat down in the booth opposite her.

"Just coffee, please," he said to the waitress who appeared immediately with a menu.

The waitress brought it, refilled Rachel's cup and went back to the counter.

When she was out of earshot Paul Gardner said somberly, "I suppose you realize, Mrs. Carey, how it makes me feel that Amy turned to Hot Line for help or reassurance or whatever it was you were able to give her that she didn't get from me. God knows I didn't take her problems as seriously as I should have, least of all the prowler."

Rachel hesitated and then said, "I didn't always take the prowler seriously myself."

"Oh?" He gave her a quick glance. "Why not?—if you don't mind my asking."

"Because she seemed so unhappy over your night classes —as if you left her alone on purpose."

"I know." His face clouded. "Poor Amy." He made a grimace as he picked up his cup and drank from it.

But not over the taste of the coffee, hot and good, Rachel thought; over some spasm of memory connected with his dead wife.

After a brief silence he continued, "I took the prowler seriously enough the first couple of times, put chains on the doors, moved my car out of sight down the street one night —we have a double carport—and stayed home from classes hoping he'd show. Did she tell you that?"

"I don't think so."

"But when she kept talking about my changing my schedule—which I couldn't do since it was already set for the spring semester—or giving up my job, I began to wonder if she wasn't making up a lot about the prowler to get her own way. She liked having it—well, everyone does but Amy more than most because her mother let her have it so much—so I dug in my heels and said no. Christ, I just said no! If I'd given in to her . . ."

"How could you possibly foresee anything like what happened?" Rachel consoled him. "No one could. I certainly didn't. Because whenever she talked about how frightened she was of the prowler it seemed to get mixed up with what had happened to her mother, including her own guilt feelings over her mother's death." She smiled ruefully. "Aren't we all amateur psychologists these days?"

"I guess so," he said. "I felt the same way."

"Then when she began concentrating on the boy down the street it seemed even less serious," Rachel continued. "Mean and cruel but not a real threat. But it went on so much, the doorbell ringing and the rapping on window-panes, that I began to wonder if it happened as often as she said it did."

"I thought that too." Paul Gardner looked a little less strained. "I even got impatient over it."

"Well, anyone would, not quite believing all of it," Rachel

said. "Tuesday night, though, it worried me when she said she was going outside to try and trap the prowler. She didn't seem afraid at all."

"Trap him how?"

"She said she had a good dark spot where she could sit and watch for him without being seen herself."

"So that's how she got herself killed." Paul Gardner turned it over in his mind. "The only reason I can think of that the prowler didn't just turn and run was that she recognized him. Then she must have been the one who ran; ran inside where he followed her and killed her."

"Unless it was a coincidence that she tried to trap him Tuesday night when he intended to get into the house anyway," Rachel suggested. "Or is that too much of a coincidence?"

"Yes. More likely that she recognized him." Paul Gardner shook his head. "What a thing to happen to Amy, of all people, with her mother dying the same way and she having it on her mind ever since."

"It's very sad." Rachel finished her coffee and reached for her check. "I must be going," she said.

"What? Oh yes, of course." He made an effort to rouse himself from his own concerns. "This has taken up half your morning, Mrs. Carey. Do you have children home waiting for you?"

"No."

"Where do you live?"

"Monroe Street. The garden apartments."

"I see. Does your husband work here in town or in Washington?" He smiled faintly. "That's leaving out Quantico and Belvoir, though."

"My husband is in Florida, Mr. Gardner, working for an uncle in the real estate business there." Rachel usually ended any reference to her husband at that point. But somehow, talking with Paul Gardner as if they were friends instead of strangers just met, it didn't seem enough. So, after a moment she added, "We're legally separated and will soon be divorced."

"Oh. I'm sorry." He signaled the waitress as he spoke and she came over carrying the steaming glass pot. Before Rachel could check her she filled her cup again and then his.

"She seems to feel you have time for another cup," he said when she was gone.

Rachel smiled. "Yes."

The door opened and a man came in looking around as if seeking someone. Seeking, it turned out, Paul Gardner, saying when he reached their booth, "Oh, here you are, Paul. I thought you might be when they told me at the police station that you'd left but your car was still in the parking lot there."

"Hi, Frank. Sit down." Paul Gardner half rose, moving over to make room for him. "Mrs. Carey, this is Frank Lambert, Amy's stepfather."

"How do you do," Rachel said.

"Mrs. Carey?" Lambert smiled at her pleasantly but made it a question.

Paul Gardner answered it. "Mrs. Carey is a Hot Line volunteer and had some information to give the police about Amy, who called her several times this winter."

"Amy called Hot Line?" Lambert, taken aback, stared at Rachel. "But—I always thought—well, isn't that for people in real trouble?"

"Not necessarily," she replied. "Your stepdaughter needed someone to talk to about the prowler."

"Oh yes." He looked grave. "I'm afraid neither one of us, Paul or I, paid enough attention to it. Maybe it was because she talked about it so much—you know, like the boy who cried wolf?"

"Yes," said Rachel, remembering that she had once had the same thought about Amy Gardner herself.

As he went on deploring their attitude, Rachel looked at him appraisingly. He was probably no more than in his late thirties—hadn't Amy Gardner said he was several years younger than her mother?—and looked even younger than he was, looked almost boyish, with a suggestion of high spirits showing on his face, in the crinkles around his mouth and eyes and in his ready smile as he caught the eye of an acquaintance across the room.

He was a handsome man with a fresh clear complexion, hazel eyes and a heavy mustache as dark as his hair; something of a fashion plate, too, everything he wore carefully selected to blend with the rest. Paul Gardner, in casual slacks and jacket, shirt open at the neck, looked thrown-together by contrast.

But he was the one who attracted Rachel.

He might be a murderer, she reminded herself.

But so might Lambert. According to Amy Gardner, there had never been any love lost between them. Not that this made a strong motive for murder, not when they hadn't even lived under the same roof since her marriage and presumably not gone out of their way to see much of each other.

But what did Rachel really know about their feelings toward each other, the stepfather and stepdaughter?

More to the point, of course, were the feelings between the Gardners themselves; when it came to murder, the husband or wife was generally assumed to have the strongest motive of all.

"Any special reason you were looking for me, Frank?" Paul Gardner asked interrupting the other's soliloquy on how tragic the whole thing was.

"Well, I'd stopped at my house on the way back to my office and your cleaning woman called and said that Mayberry was trying to reach you." Lambert's voice dropped a note as he added, "From what she said, it seems Amy's body has been released to him."

"Oh." The strained look deepened on Paul Gardner's face.

"He'd like you to drop by at the funeral home," Lambert

said. After a pause he asked, "Do you want me to go with you?"

"No thanks, I'll manage."

Lambert looked relieved.

Rachel got to her feet. "I must go now."

Both men stood up to say good-by.

"I hope we'll meet again, Mrs. Carey, under happier circumstances," Lambert said with a smile.

His mustache, she noticed, was neatly trimmed. But she didn't like mustaches.

Still, she thought, shaking hands with him and Paul Gardner, he must appeal to a lot of women.

She wondered as she left why he had never remarried; and then why his face seemed familiar even though she was sure she hadn't met him before.

Getting into her car in the police parking lot she realized suddenly she had seen his picture in the paper sometime recently. As city planner he had some connection with—was it called Urban something?—no, Downtown Revitalization Program. Meetings, statements on it, were written up regularly.

CHAPTER TEN

Rachel stopped to get books at the library but had no particular plans for the rest of the day when she arrived home around noon. Reading was for later; meanwhile, she should keep busy, she thought, do something that would take her mind off Amy Gardner.

Why not give her apartment a good cleaning? It was long overdue.

She changed into jeans and an old shirt and got to work on it.

It was almost five o'clock when she finished, waxing the kitchen floor last of all. She felt pleasantly tired and virtuous with accomplishment as she put away the cleaning equipment and went into the bathroom to wash her hands and run a comb through her hair, standing on end from her exertions.

The doorbell rang. It was Luke Welford holding her paper.

"Hi," he said handing it to her. "This just came."

"Thank you." He was so far from her thoughts at the moment that she stared at him blankly.

"Aren't you inviting me in?"

"What? Oh yes." She stood aside.

He sniffed the air as he entered the living room. "Mmm. Smells good in here. Nothing nicer than the smell of wax."

"I've cleaned the whole place," Rachel said looking around with pride. "Just shines, doesn't it?"

"It sure does. But you don't." He grinned as he took in her appearance, her grubby shirt, jeans spattered with ancient paint stains. "Kind of like the effect, though, the results of honest toil."

"Well . . ." Rachel picked up the tail of her shirt. "Not so good. I'll go put on a clean one and make us a drink."

She didn't need to ask him what he was doing in Monmouth at this unexpected hour. It had to do with Amy Gardner. He would at last tell her that he had a cousin who lived —had lived—here.

He was looking at the paper when she returned to the living room but put it down and followed her out into the kitchen in uncharacteristic silence to help with the drinks.

When they were back in the living room, settled down facing each other, Luke made a gesture of raising his glass before he drank from it and said, "*Salud*," in a faraway tone, his thoughts elsewhere.

A moment later he looked at her soberly and said, "You haven't asked me what I'm doing in Monmouth at this time of day when I should be just leaving my office."

"I already know," she replied.

His glance sharpened. "About Amy? How did you know? I don't recall ever mentioning that I had a cousin living here."

"You never did." Rachel gave him a level look. "Why not?"

He hesitated, then shrugged. "Hard to say. Maybe I should have the first time I met you and you said you lived in Monmouth. But that sort of thing always seems a bit stupid to me, the way it comes out. 'Oh, I have a cousin who lives there—Amy Gardner. Do you know her?' And as long as I didn't tell you right away there was never any particular reason to mention it later."

"I know what you mean," Rachel said swirling the ice in her glass. "Just the same, it still seems a little funny that somewhere along the way you didn't bring it up. More natural if you had."

"Sorry. I tend to compartmentalize my life, I guess. Keep

my friends and relatives apart, as it were. I thought you might know Amy—as you apparently did—and that it might lead to one of those Why-don't-we-all-get-together? deals. Which was the last thing I wanted. I hadn't seen Amy in nearly two years. Although I saw a lot of her at one time . . ."

Luke's tone was moody. He took a long swallow of his drink and continued, "Our mothers were sisters. Mine's in Greece right now with my father. I tried to call them at their hotel in Athens today but they're off touring somewhere in a car. I guess you know what happened to Aunt Stella. I used to come here on visits from Scranton and while I was at GW I came down fairly often weekends. After I graduated and started working at the agency I still came. I was very fond of Aunt Stella and fond of Amy too, although she was kind of a spoiled brat, only child and all. She was almost five years younger than me."

"Weren't you at the party with her the night her mother was killed?"

Luke gave Rachel a quizzical look. "You know a lot about us, don't you? Yes, I was. I went back to the house with Paul and her that night when Frank called."

He finished his drink and stood up. "I'm ready for a refill. What about you?"

Rachel shook her head. She had barely touched hers.

He came back with a fresh drink, sat down and continued, "Amy went all to pieces. Christ it was awful. She never really got over it, was never the same again, never any fun to be with. All the brightness drained out of her like pulling a plug to let the water out. It got so depressing after a while that I began to stay away."

"I should think she needed you more than ever then." Rachel kept her tone neutral.

"God knows I tried at first to cheer her up but it did no good. Anyway, she had Paul. He stood by her. Poor guy's been a glutton for punishment."

Fair-weather cousin, thought Rachel.

"So I stayed away more and more. Last couple of years I've hardly seen her at all." Luke, looking off into the distance, brought his gaze back to Rachel. "How long ago did she tell you we were cousins?"

"She never did. It wasn't like that at all . . ." Rachel paused but could see no way to avoid mentioning Hot Line. Paul Gardner or Lambert would tell him about it if she didn't. She was tired of repeating the story, though, and gave Luke the briefest résumé of it that she could.

"So that was it," he said. "Hot Line. And I thought—" he checked himself.

"Thought what?"

It wouldn't show much finesse to tell Rachel he had thought she was dating someone else nights she said she was busy. He brushed aside Rachel's question. "Just a stupid idea." Then, changing the subject, "Tonight's paper mentions Amy setting a trap for the prowler. I read it while you were changing your shirt."

"Does it bring in Hot Line?" Rachel stood up and went over to the table where he had left the paper.

"No. Just says something about a source close to Mrs. Gardner."

Rachel took the paper back to her chair and skimmed through the front-page story. As Luke had said, no mention of Hot Line. Mrs. Holt would be pleased over that. Well, Rachel was pleased too. She read on. Funeral services, the story concluded, would be held tomorrow but time and place were omitted.

She put the paper down and asked, "When did you hear about Amy?"

"Not until yesterday morning. Paul could have reached me Tuesday night. I was home the whole evening working on a layout for one of our clients. But he didn't think of it, he said. No reason he should, of course. He certainly had enough else on his mind."

Luke got to his feet and wandered restlessly around the room. "I couldn't get down here yesterday at all. I had an all-day meeting set up with a new client of the agency that included dinner last night. Paul understood. He said there was nothing I could do anyway. I left the office early this afternoon, though, and came down. He seems to be standing up to it pretty well. He's had plenty of practice with Amy."

"I'm sure he has," Rachel said keeping to herself the thought that except for whatever help he might have had from Franklin Lambert he had carried the weight of it alone.

Luke had stayed well out of it.

Wanting to jar him she said, "It's too bad that close as you were to Amy, you couldn't help her get over her obsession that she was to blame for her mother's death by not locking the door."

"But no one could help her on that," Luke defended himself. "She was nuts on the subject." Still pacing back and forth he came to a halt in front of Rachel. "She seems to have told you her whole life story."

"Not really. Just the particular things that haunted her."

"I should have done more," he said half to himself. "Should have tried harder to help."

"Yes, you should have," Rachel agreed and then held out her glass. "I think I'll have another drink now."

He made it for her. She drank it slowly, suddenly aware of how tired she was from the long day and lack of sleep the night before.

Luke went back to his chair. "I still can't believe it," he said. "First Aunt Stella and now Amy. Both dead, both dying the same way."

Rachel sighed. "Let's not talk about it any more for now. I've been in a state of shock since I read about it in last night's paper. I'd got fond—well, protective, I guess you'd call it—of Amy. As if I'd known her a long time."

"Just one more thing, though. How did you happen to get involved with Hot Line?"

"Through the mother of a friend who's on the board of the Mental Health Association. She suggested it and it seemed like something useful to do." Rachel, since she never talked to Luke about her husband, hesitated but then added, "I'm more or less marking time here in Monmouth, you see, until my divorce goes through. The substitute teaching I do doesn't take up enough of my time. I need to keep busy. I do other volunteer work, too, occasionally. Which means," she wound up her explanation, "I'm not exactly a goody-goody all wrapped up in helping my fellow man. I'm first of all helping myself."

"Thank heaven," Luke said with exaggerated piety and they both laughed easing the slight tension that had built up between them.

"Look," he said next getting up from his chair, "I've got to go downtown and get a haircut. Why don't you get cleaned up in the meantime—big smudge under your chin in case you didn't notice it—and we'll go out somewhere for early dinner. Then I'll drop by at Paul's again before I go back to Alexandria. A cousin of Amy's on her father's side came up from Richmond this afternoon but she should be gone by the time I get back to the house."

"That sounds good to me," Rachel said. "I don't much feel like getting my own dinner and staying here by myself."

"Any time you don't want to stay alone at night just call the Welford Service." Luke pulled her up out of her chair and held her close to him. "Lovely ladies a specialty," he murmured against her ear.

"What fee do you—?" Rachel began, but his kiss smothered her query.

She was breathless when he let her go at last, all his charm concentrated in the slow smile he gave her. "You're quite some girl, Rachel Carey," he said, and then was gone, calling from the door, "Be back as soon as I get away from the barber."

They went to the Monmouth Inn for dinner. They were quieter than usual during the meal and Luke brought her home not long after eight o'clock.

"You're going to Paul Gardner's now?" she asked at the door.

"Just for a little while. I'll be back tomorrow, though, for the funeral."

"What time is it being held and where? The paper didn't say."

"Monmouth Cemetery. Graveside service at three o'clock. There'll be a gathering of the clan afterward at Frank's." Luke bent his head and kissed her lightly. "Good night, baby. Call you soon."

"Good night," Rachel said.

Later, getting ready for bed, she made up her mind to go to the funeral herself, a gesture to mark the end of a strange but in an odd sort of way, close association. Not to leave it dangling, she thought. And also that Amy Gardner, who had only known her as Martha, might have liked the idea of her being there.

CHAPTER ELEVEN

Officer Denton of the Monmouth Police Department spent most of that Thursday afternoon ringing doorbells on Britton Road, arriving back at headquarters around five o'clock with the list of names and addresses he had compiled. He ran off several copies of it, left one with Records and took the rest to Captain Betz.

"Here you are, sir," he said, putting the original list on the desk in front of him. "Records is checking to see if they have anything on them."

"Thanks." Betz ran his eye over the list. "Fairly complete, you think?"

"Don't see how I could have missed any, sir. I covered every house on both sides of the street for four blocks from the Gardners'. Their house is at the top of an incline and there was no way to tell which direction Mrs. Gardner meant by down the street."

"Fine. That's all for now, Denton. You've put in an hour of overtime already."

When Denton left the captain counted the names on the list, a total of fifteen in all. Could be worse, he thought, picking up his phone and asking Lieutenant Wagner to come to his office.

Wagner, his assistant in the investigative division, appeared shortly.

"Sit down, Jim, and look at this," Betz said, handing him a copy of the list.

The lieutenant sat down and looked at it. "That all?" he said. "Oh, it's just those near the Gardners'. Must be a lot more than that the whole length of Britton Road out to the county line. What's the Gardners' street number? It's not on here."

The captain checked. "It's 1529."

Wagner pondered over the list. "I shouldn't think it would be the kid right next door at 1527 when she didn't know his name. Best place to start, seems to me, would be the fourteen or sixteen hundred blocks. That would be down the street going in either direction."

"Well, you figure it out," Betz told him. "All I know is, I want that kid fast. Meanwhile," he stood up, yawned and stretched, "I'm going home, grab a bite to eat, take a shower." He rubbed his face experimentally. "Need a shave too. Christ, I've hardly had a minute to call my own since this case started. Who you going to send out on it?"

"Morris."

Betz nodded. Sergeant Morris, one of the younger men, was one of the best on the force. "If anything breaks before I get back, call me at home," he said.

Soon after he left, Sergeant Morris, young, smart, something of an eager beaver and the possessor of a college degree, was on his way to Britton Road.

Just before his departure Records called to say that three of those on the list had been arrested for traffic violations within the past year.

Morris started out in the fourteen hundred block where the first name listed was Arthur Greenwood.

He rang the doorbell of the new-looking gray brick house. All the houses this far out on Britton Road were relatively new. Sergeant Morris, a native of Monmouth, remembered that when he was a kid most of the area had been open fields where he used to play. He was twenty-eight now. Time slipped by, he thought pensively, and felt old.

The man who answered the door instantly made him feel young again, a mere sprat. He looked to be in his eighties, white-haired and bent with age.

Morris presented his identification folder and asked to speak to Arthur Greenwood.

"My son Arthur or my grandson Arthur?" The old man eyed the identification folder vaguely. "Police, you said? My son's not home from his office yet."

"Your grandson, Mr. Greenwood."

"Oh. What's the boy done?"

"Nothing so far as I know, sir. Just a few questions I'd like to ask him."

"Well, I'd better let you talk to my daughter-in-law. You wait here and I'll get her."

The old man shuffled off down the hall, leaving Morris standing just inside the door sniffing the rich smell of pot roast—a reminder that he'd had an early lunch, nothing since, and normally would have been off duty by this time anticipating his own dinner. He heaved a self-pitying sigh.

Arthur's mother came from the rear of the house, her father-in-law trailing behind. She inspected Morris's identification and fixed a suspicious gaze on him while he explained the purpose of his visit.

"Does it have something to do with that girl up the street who was killed the other night?" she asked.

"Yes. Boys get around a lot and see things, Mrs. Greenwood."

"Not Arthur," she said with conviction. "I'm sure he's never talked to the girl. We've never met her or her husband. That's what I told the policeman who was around the neighborhood yesterday looking for information."

"Still, you never know, ma'am."

"Well, I'll call him although it's too bad to interrupt his homework for nothing."

She moved to the foot of the stairs and called, "Arthur! Someone to see you."

Doing his homework upstairs like the kid Mrs. Gardner had suspected. Did they have a family room out back?

"Coming, Mother," a reedy voice answered and a moment later Arthur Greenwood came down the stairs.

Morris's faint stir of hope that he had struck pay dirt at his first stop vanished as the boy came into view. Small, skinny, frail in build, he must just barely have reached his teens, Morris thought. He looked no more than eleven or twelve.

"This man is from the police department, Arthur," his mother said. "He wants to ask you some questions about Mrs. Gardner."

"Mrs. Gardner?" Arthur piped with perfect self-possession looking up at the sergeant through large round eyeglasses. "We only moved here last fall and I wasn't even sure who she was when we first heard what happened to her."

"Oh. I thought perhaps when you were out playing—"

"I don't play outside all that much," Arthur piped earnestly. "I read a lot and my tropical fish take up a lot of my time and now there's my chemistry set. It's a real super one and I've got kind of a lab fixed up in the basement trying different experiments with it. I was down there today, in fact, right after school."

He gave Morris an innocent owl-eyed look. "I was making acetylsalicylic acid."

"Acid? Couldn't you hurt yourself playing with stuff like that?"

Arthur shook his head, more innocent-looking than ever as he explained gently, "Acetylsalicylic acid is aspirin."

A smart-ass, thought Morris, chagrined that he had walked right into the trap. He returned the innocent look impassively.

"I'm going to be a chemist when I grow up," Arthur announced.

His I.Q. level was probably 150 to 160, way above Morris's, which was just high average. Maybe, though, he thought hopefully, the kid would move on from aspirin to something that would blow him up before he grew up to become president of Dow Chemical.

But he was wasting his time here, Morris thought next, taking another look at Arthur's physique. Arms and legs like twigs, the kid would hardly be able to swat a fly, let alone bludgeon anyone to death.

The sergeant reached behind him for the doorknob, expressing his thanks and getting himself out of the house as fast as he could.

The teen-ager at his next stop in the fourteen hundred block was a big broad-shouldered kid, at eye level with Morris's own six-one, strong enough, he thought, to tackle an ox, let alone a slightly built young woman.

The trouble was, it turned out, that the kid had played basketball Tuesday night until ten o'clock and afterward had gone to the Hot Shoppe for hamburgers with several of the other players. Then he had taken one of them home— he was driving his mother's car—and had not got home himself until eleven o'clock.

His parents verified the time; the eleven o'clock news had just come on when their son drove into the garage.

"He went straight up to bed," the mother volunteered, "but we watched the news. After it was over and I was locking up the house I saw a police car go by and stop up the street. Then I saw that there was another one there already. I called my husband's attention to it and we wondered what had happened but we didn't find out until the next morning."

The boy—young man was more accurate—supplied the names of the basketball players and the friend he had driven home. They would be checked as a matter of routine but Morris didn't doubt that they would verify the boy's statement.

He replied to Morris's next question by saying that he had never thrown stones at Mrs. Gardner's cat or had a run-in with her over that or anything else. He hardly knew her, in fact; just to say hello when they met.

Morris went on through the rest of the fourteen hundred block and all of the thirteen hundred block. From one address to the next he went, interrupting dinner hours. Some parents bristled at the idea that their sons should be questioned, others were co-operative; one offered him a drink. It all took time, reassuring parents and kids, framing questions carefully, trying to establish some sort of rapport with them.

By seven-thirty, working his way back on the even-numbered side of the street, he reached the sixteen hundred block beyond the Gardner house.

At least most people's dinner hour was over, he reflected, ringing the doorbell at 1654. The boy who lived there, Peter Jackson, was one of the three on the list who had a traffic violation charged against him. It was a speeding charge reduced with the aid of one of the sharpest, most expensive lawyers in town to violation of the rules of the road.

But judging by the big stone and clapboard house, his parents could afford the fee, Morris thought.

A tall gangling boy, sixteen or seventeen, with shoulder-length blond hair answered the door. He was Peter Jackson, he said, and lost color when Morris produced his identification folder.

"Come in," he said.

Morris stepped into a large front hall with a spacious living room visible through an archway on one side and a library lined with bookshelves on the other.

From somewhere in back came the sound of a television.

"What did you want to—see me about?" Peter Jackson asked, swallowing in the middle of the question.

"Just making a routine check of young people in the neighborhood," the sergeant replied.

"On account of that murder up the street?"

"Yes, we're looking for information on it. Are your parents home, Peter?"

Even as Morris asked this a woman's voice called from the back of the house, "Who is it, Peter?"

The boy had to swallow again before he called back, "It's a policeman, Mother." Then he said on a hopeful note to Morris, "You want to talk to my parents too, don't you? They're in the family room out in back."

"I'd like them to be present," Morris replied, and followed him down the hall past dining room and kitchen and around a jog into a big room spread across the back of the house.

It fitted Amy Gardner's description, Morris thought. Peter Jackson was the kid he was looking for.

The faded blonde standing in the middle of the room was his mother. His father, lean and brisk, pressed a remote control button to turn off the TV and stood up from an armchair by the fireplace where a small fire crackled.

Both parents eyed Morris as he introduced himself with a wariness they tried to conceal.

"Sit down, Sergeant," the father said.

"Thank you." Morris sat down, the mother returned to her chair and reached for her cigarette, sending up a plume of smoke from the ash tray beside it.

Peter Jackson remained standing near the doorway, leaning against the wall.

"What can we do for you?" the father asked when they were all seated.

"Just a few questions I'd like to ask Peter," Morris said and went through his little speech about boys getting around a neighborhood a lot more than older people and seeing a lot that they might miss.

"It's about Mrs. Gardner, isn't it?" The mother had a quick crisp voice that Morris categorized as a Yankee voice.

"Yes, ma'am," he said, nothing more, letting her take the lead again.

"Terrible thing," she said, shaking her head. "We were shocked when we heard about it. Not that we knew her very well. She kept to herself, never seemed to mix with her neighbors at all. Rather an odd sort of girl I was told."

"Oh. Who told you, Mrs. Jackson?"

She shrugged. "I don't remember."

Morris turned his gaze to the boy leaning against the wall. "Did you know her, Peter?"

"Well, not really."

"I just told you, Sergeant, that she kept to herself," the mother cut in. "So you see, there's really not much any of us can tell you about her, I'm afraid."

The father, filling his pipe, said nothing.

Morris let it pass. "Have you had any prowlers around your place this winter?" he asked looking at Peter Jackson who stiffened and squared his shoulders giving the effect of having his back to the wall.

"None," the father said briefly.

Morris kept his gaze on the boy. "But you did know Mrs. Gardner well enough, didn't you, Peter, to have a run-in with her about her cat?"

Before her son could speak for himself, the mother took over, exclaiming, "Do you mean to say, Sergeant, that she made a complaint to the police about a trifle like that? How petty of her! Even though she's dead now, I can't help saying it."

"Mom . . ." the boy began but his mother ignored him, sitting forward, making energetic gestures as she added, "Peter wasn't trying to hurt her cat either. He told me about it when he got home, what a mean old thing it was, hissing and snarling at him. He said he just picked up a few stones to drive it off, not meaning to hit it at all."

She turned to her son. "Isn't that right, Peter?"

"Yes," he muttered looking away from her.

"The police never came near us at the time so I felt they had sense enough not to listen to her complaints." The mother sat back with a vindicated expression and lit a fresh cigarette.

"Mrs. Gardner didn't call us at all about the cat," Morris informed her. "She did complain to us, though, three or four times about a prowler around her house. It always happened nights her husband was teaching, which made her suspect it was a neighborhood kid she'd had some trouble with. All he'd have to do, she said, was check first to make sure her husband's car wasn't in the carport."

"Well, I declare!" the mother burst out. "That wretched girl—yes, I will call her that, regardless that she's dead, because that's what she was—accusing Peter, trying to make trouble for him even though we told her the night she came here—"

"Loretta!" the father broke in, but it was too late.

Peter Jackson sagged against the wall.

Morris waited a moment and then said, "Mrs. Gardner felt that given the layout of the house Peter could slip in and out when you were out here in back without your knowing it."

"Ridiculous," the mother snapped sitting bolt upright. "As if Peter didn't have better things to do with his time than to sneak over there ringing doorbells and rapping on windows. That's what she was accusing him of the night she came here."

A sickly grin showed on Peter's face and stayed there as if set in place.

"Does your son have a TV set in his room?" Morris asked.

"Yes, but—"

"Loretta," the father said taking charge at last. He looked at his son sternly. "Peter, if you'll just tell the sergeant that he's way off base I'll ask him to leave."

Peter opened his mouth and closed it, gulping air.

"Peter . . ."

How soon did he have to warn the kid? He looked the

picture of guilt, Morris thought, and there was thin ice ahead.

"Peter . . ."

"I was only trying to scare her," the boy blurted out, "because she carried on so about her rotten old cat. You should have heard her the second time I happened to stop out front when the cat was sitting on the steps. Just because I made believe I was drawing a bead on it she came rushing out yelling at me to get away from her house and threatening that if I ever came anywhere near it again she'd call the police."

Morris felt he could wait no longer. "Peter, I must advise you that anything you say can be used against you in a court of law and that you have the constitutional right to refuse to answer any questions—"

The father sprang to his feet. "Don't say another word, son. I'm calling Grant."

Grant, Morris noted. He was the high-priced lawyer who had got Peter Jackson's speeding charge reduced to violation of the rules of the road.

"But Dad," the boy cried, "I didn't do one thing to Mrs. Gardner. Like I told you, I just wanted to scare her a little because—"

"Shut up, Peter," the father said, and went over to the phone on a nearby table.

"—or to make any statement whatsoever or, if you so choose, to have an attorney present during any interrogation," Morris droned.

"Crying out loud," Peter muttered.

"Tell him to meet us at the police station," Morris said, getting to his feet while the father talked to his lawyer.

"No, have him come here," the mother said. "I won't allow Peter to be taken to the police station. There's no need of it just over a silly prank."

The father paid no attention to her, talking in an undertone on the phone. Presently he hung up and said, "Grant will meet us there in twenty minutes."

The mother began to cry.

"Hey, cut it out, Mom," Peter said awkwardly. "It's not the end of the world. I didn't do anything so terrible."

"Outrage—no reason to—never heard of—" the mother sobbed incoherently.

"Pull yourself together, Loretta," the father said. "Grant will get this straightened out in no time. Peter, go comb your hair and get a jacket." He glanced at Morris. "We'll follow you in our car."

"Okay," said Morris.

Grant arrived soon after them, a middle-aged man who looked as if nothing in the world could ever surprise him again.

Captain Betz, back at his desk, held the interview in his office, first allowing time for Grant to confer privately with his clients.

As the interview progressed, the lawyer brushed aside the prospect of even a trespassing charge against Peter Jackson. There were no witnesses to it, no physical evidence, he pointed out; just the boy's unsupported admission that would never stand up by itself in a court of law.

There was no connection between Peter's activities and Mrs. Gardner's murder, Grant continued. He hadn't left his house Tuesday night when it took place.

The mother spoke up firmly in support of her son's alibi. She had talked to him upstairs in his room that night, shortly before nine o'clock, she said. Thereafter, for the next hour or more, the crucial time, she was at her desk in the library writing invitations to a cocktail party she was giving two weeks hence. Peter could not have come downstairs or left the house without her knowledge.

She would make a formidable witness, Morris thought, now that she had got over the first shock of her son's disclosures.

Speaking for himself, Peter Jackson insisted that he had prowled only three times altogether; that either someone else had been there or Mrs. Gardner had made up stories about the other times.

In the end Betz let him go with no charge placed against him.

"We'll see what develops," Betz said afterward to Morris. "If he's the one we're looking for, he'll feel safe now, make some move, maybe, that will give him away."

Morris looked thoughtful. "Suppose he was telling the truth about only prowling three times—what about the other times Mrs. Gardner mentioned to Mrs. Carey? Could there have been someone else who . . ."

His voice died away. Two prowlers were one too many.

But as they talked it over, neither Betz nor he was happy with Peter Jackson as the murderer.

CHAPTER TWELVE

Friday afternoon Rachel went to Amy Gardner's funeral. It occurred to her on the way that among the people who would attend her position was unique; that she was in all likelihood the last person the dead girl had talked to.

Except, of course, the murderer. They must have said something to each other before he killed her.

Would he attend her funeral?

That was an unpleasant thought.

The service was about to begin when Rachel reached the cemetery, the coffin already placed over the grave, people positioning themselves around it, not as many as she had expected there would be. But with time and place omitted from the newspaper, curiosity seekers who might otherwise have come had been kept away. Those present, she thought, were limited to the family and friends of Amy Gardner.

Rachel felt something of an intruder herself, parking her car away from the rest and standing in back when she reached the gathering.

She looked steadily at the dark wood coffin, its stark lines softened by flowers, while the minister intoned the burial service. It seemed strange to her that she should be there looking at the coffin without being able to visualize the girl inside it. The people around her could but she didn't know whether Amy Gardner was dark or fair, tall or short, fat or thin. All she had to go on was a newspaper picture and a light childish voice that gave no clue to its owner's appearance.

And yet, in a way, she had perhaps been closer to the

dead girl, as a confidante, in the last weeks of her life than most of those present.

And so not really an intruder at her funeral.

". . . And now if you will all join me in saying the Lord's Prayer," said the minister and Rachel bowed her head and repeated it with the rest.

"Ashes to ashes, dust to dust . . ." The coffin was lowered partway into the grave.

Rachel's eyes filled with tears. Poor Amy Gardner, she thought. After only twenty-three years of life, the last few shadowed by tragedy, she had come to a violent end herself.

The service was over, the group moving around, breaking up. Rachel caught sight of the three she knew, Paul Gardner, Franklin Lambert and Luke in the front row of mourners with people now approaching them to shake hands and offer sympathy.

Rachel started to leave but Luke saw her and made his way through the gathering, catching up with her just as she got into her car.

"How nice of you to come," he said. "Why didn't you tell me you were going to yesterday?"

"I didn't know it then myself. But last night I thought about it and felt I should."

"Well, now you're here why don't you join us at Frank's? Everyone's invited."

"I think not."

"Oh. Well, I must get right back myself. I'll be in touch."

Luke stood there while she backed her car around and drove away.

Unexpectedly, Rachel began to cry on the way home and knew that her tears were for herself as well as Amy Gardner.

Drinks and sandwiches and coffee were ready for the funeral guests who went to Lambert's house afterward. The social amenities were observed but there was not as much talk and laughter as there would have been if Amy Gardner had died a natural death. No one stayed as long as they might have, either, although Lambert was an excellent host, looking after everyone's needs.

By five-thirty the last car drove off leaving only Paul Gardner and Luke still present.

"Thank God it's over and now I can go home myself," Paul Gardner said.

"No indeed." Lambert got up from his chair and went over to the bar. "Let's have a drink. Then I'd like you both to stay on for an early cold supper. No," as they both started to refuse, "I won't let you go. In a time of trouble families should stick together. Besides, Ruby's feelings would be hurt. She baked a ham yesterday—and who'd turn down one of her hams?—and she's out there in the kitchen now, slicing it, probably, and fixing a salad. She's got that helper I brought in with her. I told her to have the girl set the table and we'd take care of ourselves."

The two younger men looked at each other resignedly. There was no way to turn him down.

At that moment, as if to reinforce his invitation, Ruby stuck her head in the door and said, "Mistuh Frank, I just set a pan of biscuits in the refrigerator. Ten minutes or so before you-all are ready to eat you turn the oven on and pop them in. Temperature's set for them. Everything else is ready."

"Thank you, Ruby."

"You're welcome. Oh, fixed the percolatuh too. Just plug it in. Plenty of cakes and pies, too, that the neighbuhs brought in."

"We'll be fine, Ruby. You run along home now and take the helper with you. See you in the morning."

They said good night to her and a few minutes later heard her car go down the driveway.

"Don't know what I'd do without her," Lambert said walking drink in hand to the French door.

The same French door, Paul Gardner reflected, that Amy had forgotten to lock the night her mother was killed.

He was tired. He slouched low in the big comfortable chair, sipping his drink, letting his thoughts settle on that October night nearly three and a half years ago when Amy, glowing with happiness, answered his ring at the door.

She had looked her best that night in a long blue dress with a high neckline that framed her face, deepening the clear ivory pallor of her complexion. She never used rouge or, for that matter, much make-up of any kind. Something on her eyes, perhaps, but that was all.

She had lovely dark eyes. So did Rachel Carey. Hers were very clear and steady, even darker than Amy's, a deep velvet brown . . . But what put that into his head? Well, probably Luke's mentioning that she had been at the funeral. He hadn't seen her himself. Hadn't really noticed anyone much. Had just got through it all somehow . . .

He roused himself as Lambert asked if he'd like his drink sweetened. "No thanks," he said. "Haven't really thanked you, have I, Frank, for taking over today? Very kind of you. I don't think I could have faced having them all back at our—my place."

"Glad to do it," Lambert replied and resumed his conversation with Luke Welford about public relations involved in the Downtown Revitalization Program.

Paul Gardner lapsed back into his reverie, still centered on the night Amy's mother was killed.

He hadn't seen her himself when he arrived although she had called down a greeting from upstairs. She was so worn out from a busy day, Amy said, that she had gone up to her room right after Frank left for some meeting or other and was already in bed reading.

Amy had chatted brightly as she collected her fur stole, evening bag and gloves. See, she had said putting on the gloves, I'm practicing being a proper young matron. Actually, Mother said I should wear them tonight, pay Beth the courtesy of being dressed to the nines for her party.

After that Amy had said something about what fun she and her mother had just had looking over old pieces of jewelry.

Lamps were lighted in the living room and hall but the rest of the downstairs was in darkness. Light slanted across the upstairs hall through the open door of Mrs. Lambert's bedroom.

Oh, Mother said to tell you we must try not to be too late getting home tonight because I'm having the last fitting on my dress at nine o'clock tomorrow morning.

Mother said . . . How often those words were on Amy's lips . . .

Don't forget to lock the door, dear, Mrs. Lambert called down.

No, Mother, I won't, Amy answered.

But the phone rang just then. Amy picked it up there in the hall, some call of no consequence, but she kept talking while he kept pointing to his watch to remind her that they were already making a late start.

At last she hung up and rushed to the door, her mother calling for the last time to say she hoped they would enjoy the party.

They hurried out to his car, he checking to make sure the front door was locked behind them.

Well, they had enjoyed the party. They were having a fine time until the phone rang sometime before eleven and it was Frank calling . . .

He had asked to speak to Paul, not Amy, and had told him that he'd just got in and found his wife dead in the upstairs hall.

Paul had sought out Luke first. All he told Amy was that her mother had been injured.

The police were already there when they reached the house after a tense hectic ride. Then, getting out of the car, he told Amy her mother was dead. She began screaming, neither he nor Luke, pulling up behind them in his car, able to hold her as she flew up the front steps and pounded with both fists on the door.

Frank opened it, white-faced but in fair control of himself.

No one could control Amy. She had raced upstairs, pushed a police officer aside and flung herself on her mother's body.

They'd had to call the family doctor to give her a sedative and get her to bed.

Those terrible desperate screams tearing out of her throat . . .

Not just from grief and shock, he was to learn to his sorrow. There was also the panic of a child robbed of its mother, the rock to which it clung.

In the first weeks when her frantic grief was deepened by self-blame over the unlocked door he had given Amy what comfort he could, allowing her to transfer her dependency to him, letting himself become her substitute refuge.

But by the time their postponed wedding took place uneasiness was growing in him. He no longer felt sure that as time passed Amy would get over what had happened, learn to accept as everyone who achieved maturity had to, that a hazard of loving was the possible loss of the object of that love.

Amy never had.

She had stifled him with her constant need of attention and reassurance that he loved her.

And thereby, in the end, had killed that love, leaving only a sense of duty . . .

Franklin Lambert's memories of Amy went back much farther than her husband's, back to the days when he was new in town, Monmouth's first full-time city planner, and began courting her mother.

Settling the others at the table, serving the ham, he let his memories take over . . .

Amy was twelve or thirteen when he met her, a small slight child looking up at him from under her bangs with cool self-contained rudeness.

Her mother had spoiled her rotten . . .

Her mother . . . He had fallen for her at first sight. He had barely turned thirty then, she was nearly thirty-seven, looking years younger, though, in the prime of her beauty, all sparkle and gaiety, outshining every other woman at the dance where they met.

Stella with her ash blond hair, her laughter, her willful charm . . .

Amy was away the first time he went to the house—this house which had startled him with its size and elegance, almost a mansion in his eyes compared to his own relatively modest background—but which he now took for granted as his own. Not really, of course, Stella had left him only the life use of it, but still, that was all he needed or cared about. He did not expect to marry again or have children of his own.

He would never love another woman as he had loved Stella . . .

The second time he took Stella out he met Amy. He tried to be nice to her but it was no use. She hardly spoke and then made a fuss over something to delay their going out. Nothing personal, Stella told him later, shrugging it off, it was just that she was jealous of any man who looked twice at her mother.

He had never been able to overcome Amy's hostility. It endured even after Stella's death right up until her own.

She had never wanted to share her mother with anyone.

He had made a last attempt to talk to her not long after he and Stella were married, pointing out that they weren't supposed to compete for Stella's attention, that both of them loved her, wanted to make her happy and so should try to get along together.

That talk did no more good than his earlier efforts to win Amy's friendship.

Perverse, moody kid that she was, she had been like a death's-head at the feast of his marriage.

The good days came when Stella sent her off to boarding school and then to college for two years before she gave it up to marry Paul. She came home vacations, of course, but at least the worst of the scenes stopped as she got older and more civilized.

God, how he had looked forward to getting her married and out of the house for good, just Stella and he living there together. The plans he had made for the two of them.

Plans blown sky high in the end. He couldn't believe it that night looking at Stella lying dead there on the floor.

And then there was Amy screeching at him that he shouldn't have left her mother all alone to go to a meeting, accusing, blaming him, carrying on until the doctor knocked her out with a hypo.

Stella. His beautiful Stella, who in some ways, more sophisticated, indirect ways, was as spoiled and perverse as her daughter.

But gay and lighthearted. Amy at her best was only a pale shadow of her mother but striving always to live up to her while he was often caught in the middle of their complicated relationship.

For Stella's sake, though, he had been prepared to try to feel affection for Amy if she had ever let him.

But she never had . . .

Luke Welford's memories of Amy went back farthest of all. Sitting at the table eating the excellent cold supper Ruby had left ready for them—Lord, she had been cooking good meals in this house as far back as he could remember—his thoughts, too, were on Amy.

She'd been a baby the first memory he had of her, he him-

self around five at the time, coming from Scranton with his
parents to visit Aunt Stella and Uncle Richard over some
holiday or other and there she was in her bassinet, Amy
Harriet Lundy, about three months old.

The next thing he remembered she was in pigtails, around
five herself, a perfect pest, tagging after him whenever their
two families visited each other.

Luke knew now that what he had resented most about
Amy in those days was the constant demands she made for
her mother's attention, especially after her father's death.
He had wanted his aunt Stella to himself, having fallen head
over heels in love with her when he was in first or second
grade, an infatuation that had lasted into his teens when he
built incestuous fantasies around her. Aunt Stella had been
amused and perhaps flattered by the depth of his devotion.
It had served to develop a special rapport between them
that had endured right up until her death.

That last night, that nightmare night, he had been asked
to dinner here before the party but had not been able to
make it; in fact, he had barely got to the party, arriving only
a short time before the phone call from Frank . . .

A funny kind of thing looking back on it, Luke reflected,
that Amy should have been his adoring shadow and he her
mother's.

He was at GW when Aunt Stella married Frank. It didn't
change their special relationship. She often invited him to
come down from Washington for the weekend and Amy—
about thirteen then, wasn't she?—began forcing herself into
his confidence, spilling out her jealousy and resentment of
Frank, leaning on him as much as he would let her. It had
been a burden for a kid of eighteen as he was then but it had
also made him feel quite the man of the world, cautioning
her to play it cool, not to antagonize Frank too much.

Well, she hadn't taken his advice. She had made things so
rough for the three of them that she'd finally found herself shipped off to boarding school.

His own relationship with Amy changed the summer before she went to Mary Baldwin. She had grown up, at least on the surface, and he himself was out of college working for the agency in Washington. He took her places, they were together a lot and it all led to that crazy episode . . .

Nothing came of it, thank God, and Aunt Stella never knew.

Amy left for Mary Baldwin that fall. College seemed to help her get her mother-fixation under control and show more civility to Frank, particularly after she met Paul and they started going together.

Everything was fine until the night of Aunt Stella's death . . .

Jesus, that was a night he'd never forget, Amy turned into a madwoman.

She had never been the same again. He had tried at first to do what he could but hell, a man could try just so long. It hadn't helped, either, to be around Amy, when he had his own mourning for Aunt Stella to put behind him. As much as he had loved her, it hadn't been easy.

Beautiful Aunt Stella, lying in a pool of blood, the back of her head crushed in. And her blood all over Amy when they finally lifted her off her mother's body.

Now Amy had died the same way herself.

God . . . A chill ran through Luke. He picked up the wineglass Lambert had just refilled and took a hasty gulp from it.

CHAPTER THIRTEEN

"Like I told you twenty times already, Miz Gardner, she gave it to me herself," Albert Corley said.

He had been saying it for over two hours, ever since they had picked him up at Southworth Jewelers where he had tried to sell a ring belonging to Amy Gardner.

They had circulated, without much hope, a description of her missing jewelry, supplied by the insurance agent, among the local stores. That was on Friday, the day of her funeral, only three days ago.

Today, Monday, Corley, who did yardwork for the Gardners, had walked into the jewelry store and asked how much they would give him for the ring, a 1.40 carat diamond set in platinum that turned out to be Amy Gardner's engagement ring. Southworth had gone into his office and called the police.

Corley had been picked up outside the store, the unsold ring in his pocket, and maintained steadfastly that the dead girl had given him the ring.

Now they had a search warrant and two officers had been sent to search the yardman's basement apartment for the other missing pieces of jewelry.

Meanwhile, he not only insisted that the ring was a gift but that he had no knowledge of Amy Gardner's murder. He had been home watching a movie that night from eight-thirty to ten-thirty. Alone, yes. He spent most evenings alone. He had not gone near the Gardners' house. He had never been inside it, in fact, except to step into the kitchen to get his pay.

Betz had already established that Corley, forty-five years old, was unmarried and lived alone; that he came from Baltimore originally and had been a Monmouth resident for the past eleven years; that he worked for the park department two days a week and for people like the Gardners the rest of the time.

He had no police record in Monmouth. It would take time to hear from Baltimore. He said he had no record there either, that he'd never been in trouble with the police in his life. Warned of his right to remain silent or to have a lawyer present, he had stated firmly that he didn't need one.

"I ain't done nothing wrong," he had said. "I got nothing to hide."

According to Southworth's appraisal the ring was worth well over a thousand dollars.

Betz glanced at Sergeant Morris in a corner taking notes, sighed in exasperation and said, "All right, Corley, just tell us the whole story again."

"How many more times do I have to tell you I dint steal the ring, Miz Gardner gave it to me?"

"Well, one more time anyway."

It was Corley's turn to sigh on a long-suffering note.

"Okay," he began. "Like I said, it was Wednesday, week before last, my regular day there. I spent the morning raking the yard, cleaning things up generally. Miz Gardner, she went out all dressed up before noon. I ate the lunch I brought with me on the back steps. By the time she got home, half past two, maybe, I was pretty well finished, starting to bag everything and load it into my pickup truck to take to the dump. I was watching for Mr. Gardner, he usually gets home early Wednesday but he dint that day. There was some transplanting he'd talked about and I thought maybe he told Miz Gardner what it was so I went to the back door and rang the bell.

"She looked like she'd been crying when she came to the door and real mad too. She said it would have to wait, whatever her husband wanted me to do, because he just called and told her something came up at that college where he teaches and he wouldn't be home till late.

"She was wearing the ring she gave me and it was flashing in the sun. She was acting so funny that just trying to change the subject I said what a pretty ring it was, one of the prettiest I ever seen.

"Miz Gardner, she looked at it like she never seen it herself before and said, 'You think so? Well then, you can have it.' And she yanked it off her finger and shoved it right in my hand."

Corley recited rather than told the story, the virtuous indignation that had enlivened it the first few times drained out of his voice by repetition.

"I couldn't believe she meant it," he continued. "You could of knocked me over with a feather. I said, 'You ain't serious, Miz Gardner, are you?' And she said, 'Yes, I am. Keep it. I never want to see it again.' And she went back in the house and shut the door."

"And you kept it," said Betz.

"Well, she gave it to me, dint she? But when I got home I just put it away. I knew it was her engagement ring from her husband and that she gave it to me to spite him because she was so mad at him that day. When they made up, I thought, she'd ask it back. So I just put it away. After she was killed, though, I figured it belonged to me and I might as well find out how much I could get for it."

"Look," said Betz, "if we assume—which I don't for one minute—that you're telling the truth, Corley, you admit yourself that Mrs. Gardner gave you the ring in a fit of temper and would have asked for it back if she had lived."

"There's no way to be sure of that," Corley retorted. "She wasn't killed for nearly a week after she gave it to me. She couldn't of been mad at her husband the whole time, could she? I got a telephone. She wanted it back, whyn't she call me?"

"Because she never gave it to you in the first place," Betz said flatly. "That story of yours is unbelievable. Preposterous."

But in the back of his mind as he spoke was awareness that he shouldn't use words like that after all his years on the police force. Nothing was too unbelievable, too preposterous for people, some people, to do.

A knock on his door interrupted his thoughts. "Come in," he said.

The officer who came in laid a note on his desk, said, "Lieutenant Wagner wants you to see this, sir," and withdrew.

Betz opened it. It read, "Search completed. No other pieces of jewelry, nothing of a suspicious nature found in Corley's apartment."

Betz rallied from the setback. Corley could still have the rest of the jewelry and have stashed it away somewhere else.

In that case, though, why be in such a hurry to sell the ring, the most valuable of the missing items, right here in Monmouth?

Following the same line of thought Corley demanded, "If I killed Miz Gardner and stole her jewelry, you think I'm dumb enough to go to Southworth's and try to sell that ring?"

Betz looked at him, a big heavily built man, his face set in sullen lines. He was dumb all right but probably not that dumb.

They could charge him with theft but if he stuck to his story they couldn't make it stand up in court, not without more evidence than they had now.

Hell of a note. Two murder suspects so far and they couldn't even charge one with trespassing or, as things stood, convict the other of theft.

Not yet anyway.

"We'll have to ask you to wait, Mr. Corley." The captain

made a ceremony of the mister and added to Morris, "Have someone look after him, Sergeant."

Which meant, Morris interpreted, put him under guard in one of the interrogation rooms.

"Yessir."

"Then come back here."

"Yessir."

When he was alone Betz looked up Rachel's number and called her.

She answered on the third ring.

"Captain Betz, Mrs. Carey," he said. "I've got a question for you."

"Yes?"

"Did Mrs. Gardner ever mention a man who worked in her yard? Name is Corley whether she brought that into it or not."

Rachel gave it thought. "I don't think so. The only mention of her yard that I recall was her saying the last time we talked to each other that she had been working outdoors herself that day. But nothing about anyone else being there."

Morris knocked and was told to come in. When he saw that his superior was on the phone he sat down and waited.

Betz accepted the fact that there would be no verification of Corley's improbable story from Rachel and took another tack.

"This resentment of her husband that she kept bringing up, Mrs. Carey," he began. "Would you say that in a fit of temper at him she might give away her engagement ring, a fairly valuable one, just to get even with him or something like that?"

"You mean to a man who worked for her, not a friend?"

"Yes. I know you can't give me any real answer to it but I'd like your opinion—horseback opinion, let's call it."

There was silence at Rachel's end of the line while she went back over her conversations with Amy Gardner. Then she said slowly, "I think she might, considering how impulsive she was. And that if she did, she would be more likely to give it to her yardman than to a friend. If it were a friend, she couldn't ask for it back but with her yardman she could, offering something less valuable in its place."

"Yes, if it happened the way it was told to me and if she lived long enough to." Betz paused. "Well, thanks anyway, Mrs. Carey, for giving me your opinion."

Rachel laughed. "Horseback opinion, don't forget."

"There are worse ones," he told her, said good-by and hung up.

He looked at Morris. "I reckon you realize that was Mrs. Carey?"

"Yessir."

"She doesn't think it's too far out that Mrs. Gardner might have handed over her ring to Corley knowing she could get it back." He shook his head and brooded. "Son of a bitch of a case. A kid and a gardener for suspects. And I'm not crazy about either of them."

"You were starting to tell me about the family wills when they brought Corley in," Morris reminded him.

"Oh yes." Betz reached for his notes. "Mrs. Gardner's was very simple, a joint will with her husband leaving everything they had to each other. The mother's is more interesting. Her lawyer is going to send us a copy of it. Meanwhile, though, we hit the high spots on the phone.

"Let's begin with Mrs. Lambert's house. She left it to her daughter—it was her first husband's family home—with the provision that Lambert was to have life use of it. Lot of ifs, ands and buts attached, of course, in case circumstances changed and he wanted to sell out his interest to the daughter or something like that."

"So now he'll be dealing with Gardner on it, won't he?" Morris asked.

"Yes. There was an antenuptial agreement signed by Lambert and his wife at the time of their marriage waiving all rights in each other's estates. Lambert, from what the law-yer said, didn't have too much money anyway. The agree-ment was mostly to protect her."

Betz consulted his notes. "Regardless of it, though, Mrs. Lambert left her husband a bequest of twenty-five thousand along with life use of the house."

"And Mrs. Gardner?" Morris put in.

"I'm coming to that. She was to inherit fifty thousand out-right from her father when she was twenty-one. Her mother advanced most of it to her—she wouldn't be twenty-one un-til the following summer—so that she and Gardner could build their house before they were married."

Betz turned to the next page of his notes. "That's the background," he said. "Mrs. Lambert's total estate, includ-ing the house, antiques and such, amounted to four hundred and sixty-five thousand. Along with the bequest to Lambert there were smaller ones, servants, charities and so forth. One of them, incidentally, was ten thousand to a nephew, Lucas Welford, who lives in Alexandria."

"Mrs. Gardner's cousin then," said Morris. "First we've heard of him. And living not too far away. Shouldn't he be looked into?"

"Oh yes," Betz agreed and went on, "According to the lawyer, assets in the estate, not counting the house, came to around two hundred and ninety thousand after all be-quests, taxes and other expenses were taken care of.

"Mrs. Gardner inherited half of it when she became twenty-one. The other half of it was to be held in trust for her until she reached her twenty-fifth birthday with the in-come from it going to her in the meantime."

Betz glanced up from his notes. "You following this all right? Easier when it's right in front of you."

"I think I've got it so far," Morris replied.

"Well then . . . in the event that Mrs. Gardner died with-out issue before her twenty-fifth birthday, the half that was in trust for her was to be divided into four parts; one fourth to Lambert, one fourth to Welford, one fourth to her sister, Mrs. Dorothy Welford—must be his mother—and the remaining fourth to different charities."

Morris did arithmetic in his head. "Comes out at least thirty-five thousand each," he said. "Gardner's not exactly on the short end of the stick either. He's got the fifty-thousand-dollar house they built and whatever is left of the other half of the estate that Mrs. Gardner inherited when she was twenty-one. That's leaving out the mother's house. When Lambert dies he'll get that too."

"Oh, he did all right," Betz conceded. "Not as well as he would have, though, if Mrs. Gardner had lived another fifteen months or so until she was twenty-five."

"Except that their marriage might have fallen apart by that time," Morris pointed out. "It didn't seem to be going too well. At least I don't know any contented wives who are calling Hot Line all the time. Maybe Gardner figured he'd better settle for a bird in the hand, half a loaf, whatever you want to call it."

"He could have," said Betz. "But while we're talking about money as a motive, let's not forget that what Lambert and Welford inherit isn't exactly peanuts either."

It crossed his mind as he spoke that compared to the sums they were discussing the diamond ring in Corley's possession and Peter Jackson's adolescent tricks, unpleasant though they were, paled into insignificance.

"Lambert's got an awfully good alibi," Morris commented.

"I never like them."

"Still, he's got it. That dinner meeting he went to didn't break up until ten and he stayed on in the bar at the Lafayette Inn until after eleven with three or four guys, reputable citizens, to vouch for him."

"True," said Betz. "Gardner's isn't worth a damn, though, once you allow ten or fifteen minutes' leeway on the time of death. Doesn't take long to bash someone's head in." He paused. "We'll have to see what we can find out about Welford too."

Husband, stepfather, cousin, all benefiting financially from Amy Gardner's death, thought Morris. And, for all they knew yet, one of them might have had an additional motive for killing her. Money, though, usually stood out the most.

Betz voiced what his subordinate was thinking. "Y'know," he said, "whenever there's a lot of money involved it's hard to look beyond it. But we have to. There's Corley now, the rest of the missing jewelry and the Jackson kid."

Morris tried to look interested. Corley was a new factor but during the past few days they had been investigating Peter Jackson back to his early childhood. So far all they had come up with was a neighbor who blamed him for the disappearance of her cat a year ago, saying that he had been teasing it a lot at the time.

"Kid's got some kind of a quirk about cats," Morris said. "God knows what else is mixed up in it."

He spoke without conviction. His heart wasn't in it.

CHAPTER FOURTEEN

"I don't like the way you're involved in it, Rachel," Celia said, as they lingered over coffee and discussed the murder of Amy Gardner buried eight days ago.

They had been shopping in Washington that Saturday morning, Rachel having driven up early to help her sister pick out a dress for a dinner party she and her husband were attending that night. Celia had at last found just what she wanted in a shop on Connecticut Avenue and they had now come to the end of a late lunch in a quiet little restaurant away from the tourist beat.

Rachel shrugged in resignation over her sister's remark. "I didn't have much choice," she said. "I could hardly keep to myself what I knew about Amy Gardner after she was murdered."

Celia had no answer to that but a frown puckered her forehead as she looked at Rachel across the table from her. "Well, I just wish it had been some other Hot Line aide the girl had got attached to," she said. "Someone with a husband or family to look after her. After all, the murderer hasn't been caught yet. If it was that yardman the police captain called you about he would have been arrested by this time."

"I doubt they think he's the prowler," Rachel said. "And that's who they're looking for."

"They can't just be concentrating on him," Celia objected. "That would be putting all their eggs in one basket. They're probably doing a lot of checking on her husband and relatives like Luke Welford and the stepfather."

"I don't know much about the stepfather but I can't think of any motive Luke would have to kill her." Rachel kept her tone dispassionate, not letting irritation show that Celia, unimpressed with Luke, had been so quick to bring him into it. "He's hardly seen Amy Gardner the past two years or so. She told me that herself."

"He's her cousin," Celia stated firmly. "They used to be close, you said, and who knows what kind of problems came up between them? To say nothing of his never mentioning her to you. That seems very peculiar to me."

The only way to defend Luke, Rachel realized, was to pass on the explanation he had given her. The words came back: Not wanting to get involved in the event that she knew Amy Gardner; steering clear of her himself because she was so changed, so dreary to be with nowadays . . .

It wasn't an explanation that would raise Luke in her sister's esteem. Rachel kept it to herself.

Half an hour later she dropped Celia off outside her apartment and went on home, not able to dismiss completely her sister's parting admonition, "You just be careful now, Rachel, until this thing is cleared up."

She was involved to some extent; there was no getting around that. Last night she had finished going through the daily sheets for the past two months, listing Amy Gardner's calls by the date and time.

There were ten of them in all, eight taken by her, two by other aides.

When she arrived home she called Captain Betz to give him her findings. He wasn't in and her call was transferred to Sergeant Morris who took down the information and said that the captain would get in touch with her if he had any questions on it.

She had signed her statement days ago. Now that she had made out the list her good citizen's duty was done, Rachel thought with relief as she hung up.

Luke Welford called her a few minutes later. "Well, home

at last," he said. "I tried to get you this morning when I couldn't reach you last night. I remembered it was one of your good Samaritan nights at Hot Line and thought of calling you there but I wasn't sure it was such a good idea."

"Indeed not."

"Tonight's Saturday night. You know, date night. I thought we might get together, find something to do."

It was time she entertained him. Rachel gave quick thought to what she could give him for dinner. There were steaks in the freezer, she could run out for fresh mushrooms, make a salad . . .

"Why not have dinner here?" she suggested.

"Love to," he replied promptly. "What time—before you change your mind?"

Rachel laughed. "Oh, around six-thirty."

"Be there on the dot," he said.

How chipper he had sounded, Rachel thought a few minutes later on her way to the store. No one would guess, hearing him, that a cousin he had grown up with had been brutally murdered only a short time ago.

He seemed just as chipper when he arrived, looking at his watch when she opened the door, announcing cheerfully, "It's only six twenty-nine, Rachel, a minute to go. Shall I wait out here in the hall?"

"Not worth it," she said. "By the time I shut the door, go back inside and you ring again it will be six-thirty on the dot. You might as well come in now."

It was warm enough to eat on the balcony. She had set the table there and lighted a fire of charcoal briquettes in the hibachi. It was just beginning to glow red. There was plenty of time to serve drinks before it would be ready for broiling steaks.

Rachel's apartment was at the rear of the building, her balcony overlooking a strip of woodland and small pond where the peepers had begun their nightly chorus at the approach of dusk.

Luke's lighthearted mood lasted through dinner and afterward when the warm spring night still kept them outside, Rachel clearing the table and bringing out a bottle of cognac. But when it turned cooler and she went inside to get a sweater and change the records on the stereo she found Luke in a different mood on her return. The light from the living room showed a morose look on his face, all the earlier gaiety vanished.

He reached for the bottle of brandy, filled both their glasses and said, "I had a call from your captain Betz this afternoon. Wanted to see me Monday but I'm going to be in Baltimore all day so I told him I'd leave early Tuesday afternoon and be at the police station at three o'clock."

"He must be talking to everyone who had any connection with Amy," Rachel commented.

"Probably. Except that everyone," Luke gave her a brief glance, "didn't have a cash motive for killing her. As I had. And, of course, Paul and Frank Lambert."

"Oh?"

He explained the terms of his aunt's will. "So you see," he continued, "if Amy had lived until her twenty-fifth birthday, a year from this June, I'd be out of it. So would Frank. As it is . . . well, people get killed for a lot smaller inheritances than something close to forty thousand."

"But you were—didn't you say you were home the whole evening working on some sort of layout for one of your clients?"

"Yes." Another brief glance. "You have a good memory, girl. Maybe you were cut out to be a detective yourself."

"Hardly," she said, annoyed by the remark, feeling that it made her seem suspicious-minded. "I just happened to remember it."

"Well, anyway, it's not an alibi Betz will go for. He'll think in terms of my driving down here, killing Amy and whipping back to my apartment with no one the wiser. It could be done in less than two hours if I didn't waste any time over it."

"But, Luke, how can he think that way? The prowler—"

"You don't suppose he's concentrating all his attention in that direction, do you?"

Celia had said the same thing that afternoon, Rachel recalled. It gave her an uneasy feeling.

They were both silent for an interval listening to "Rhapsody in Blue" pouring out from the living room.

At last, in a reflective tone tinged with melancholy, Luke said, "Amy's been on my mind a lot lately."

"I'm sure she has. Childhood memories, things like that."

"Grown-up memories too. Particularly from the summer before she went to Mary Baldwin. I was a year out of college then, working at the agency, coming down to Aunt Stella's quite often for the weekend. Amy, in case I never mentioned it to you, had always had kind of a crush on me from the time she was a little kid—you know, the older cousin?—but that summer things changed a bit. She seemed more grown-up, more style, more fun to be with. We got to be good friends and went quite a few places together . . ."

Luke paused. "God, I don't know why I'm telling you all this, Rachel. Probably because it's been on my mind so much since her death." He picked up the brandy bottle. "You want some more?"

"Not right now."

He filled his glass and drank. "To this day I can't imagine how it happened but early in August I came down one weekend and Aunt Stella and Frank went somewhere leaving us alone in the house. We were out by the pool fooling around and the next thing I knew we were in bed together."

Luke came to a halt and looked at Rachel as if expecting comment. She said nothing.

He drained his glass, set it down. "It was crazy," he went on, his voice hardening. "First cousins, more like brother and sister all our lives. But it lasted for over a month, right up until she left for college. The chances we took—Amy had this reckless, what-the-hell streak that used to scare me sometimes. Because if we'd ever got caught—"

"Or if she had got pregnant," Rachel said her voice without inflection.

"No danger of that. She was on the pill. I didn't exactly seduce her, you know. It was sort of a mutual thing."

But still, Rachel thought, Amy was only eighteen and had a crush on her good-looking older cousin.

"I was more relieved than anything else when it ended," Luke continued presently. "All along in the back of my mind was this worry about what would happen if Aunt Stella found out. To tell the truth, she always meant more to me, you see, than Amy ever had or could. I was nuts about Aunt Stella from the time I was a little kid myself. God knows what she would have done. Raised hell for sure. Told my parents maybe and never let me in her house again. It would have been one hell of a mess."

"But it didn't happen," Rachel said in the same uninflected tone.

"No. We were lucky. Amy was ready to take up where we left off when she came home for Christmas vacation but I wanted no part of it. I went home over Christmas myself and only saw her a couple of times. One of those times I took her out to dinner and told her we couldn't start it all up again; that just because we got away with it in the summer was no reason to push our luck."

"What did Amy say?" Rachel asked.

"She got mad at first, hurt feelings, reproaches, the whole bit. But when she calmed down she knew I was right. Fortunately, she met some guy she liked that winter and the thing died a natural death. I helped it along by staying away all I could when she came home. The end of her sophomore year she met Paul and fell for him like a ton of bricks. Boy, that was a relief. It had me worried long after it was over that she still might let something out to Aunt Stella. She was the most unpredictable girl."

And why not, Rachel thought, rejected like that?

Amy Gardner seemed to have met quite a bit of rejection in her short life.

"You shocked?" Luke turned sidewise in his chair trying to interpret Rachel's expression in the faint light.

"Not really—except for the cousin relationship." She didn't add that almost as bad was his betrayal of his aunt's affection and trust.

He hadn't said that this had ever troubled him. His chief concern had been that he mustn't get caught.

"I shouldn't have told you," he said.

"You needed to tell someone, I guess." Rachel spoke matter-of-factly, keeping to herself the thought that he must be having belated pangs over the unsavory episode or he wouldn't have brought it up at all.

No more was said about it. Luke left a little later, thanking her for dinner, kissing her good night almost absently as if still in the thrall of old memories. At the door, though, he gave her a questioning look. "See you soon?"

"Give me a call."

"Indeed yes." A fleeting smile. "Just so long as I'm not cast into the outer darkness to repent unburdening myself of my sins."

"Confession's supposed to be good for the soul," she reminded him with a smile.

But the smile died as she closed the door. Cleaning up from dinner, Rachel reviewed all that he had told her from the money he would now inherit to the new light he had cast on his relationship with his cousin Amy.

It had given Amy a certain claim on him, hadn't it? But he had brushed it off.

Starting the dishwasher, Rachel's thoughts reverted again to the money he would get because Amy was dead.

He had been home alone working the night she was killed.

Or so he said . . .

That was a horrible thought.

But it wouldn't go away.

CHAPTER FIFTEEN

"Hot Line, this is Martha," Rachel said. "Can I help you?"

"Well, I'm not the one who needs help," the woman calling said. "It's a friend who felt a little funny about calling herself."

A friend. It was a familiar subterfuge.

"She has this daughter who's been working at a dress shop here since she graduated from high school last year. No problems there but home—that's a different story."

"In what way?"

"Well, now that she's earning her own money and been paying a little board, too, she feels she can come and go as she pleases, stay out till all hours and so on. The mother, a widow, doesn't think it's right."

"It's a stage lots of young people go through," Rachel replied keeping to the middle ground.

"But that doesn't make it right," the woman said. "And I—the mother, I mean—has been having a lot of words with the girl over it. Friday night they had a big argument and later, while the mother was out grocery shopping, the girl packed most of her clothes and took off. Didn't leave a note or anything. Saturday morning the mother called the dress shop and they said the girl had quit her job Friday night without giving any notice."

"Did she have a boy friend?"

"That was part of the trouble. He's no good. But when I—the mother tried to tell her that she wouldn't listen. She was crazy about him and nothing could change her."

"Has the mother tried to get in touch with him?"

"Oh yes. He claims he doesn't know where she is and hasn't heard from her."

"Does the girl have a car?"

"No, not yet. She's been saving to buy one, though." The woman sighed heavily. "Just think, she's been gone since Friday, this is Tuesday and that's four days without any word from her. Like she just vanished from the earth. Well, not exactly. Her bankbook is gone so she has that money, nearly two hundred dollars, and her week's pay too. So she's not penniless anyway. What I'd like to know is what can be done about it? She's only eighteen years old."

"Not much, I'm afraid," Rachel replied. "She's legally of age, self-supporting and apparently left home of her own free will since she packed her clothes and gave up her job." Rachel enumerated these points slowly to make sure the woman understood them. Then she added, "Your friend can call the police, of course, and ask them for help."

"She wouldn't want to do that. The publicity and all."

"There needn't be any. They'd just check around a little, the bus station, the railroad station, perhaps talk to her boy friend. They might be able to pick up some information for you."

"I hoped Hot Line could tell me something else—to pass on to my friend."

"I'm sorry but there really isn't anything else. You might be able to convince your friend, though, that she would feel better if the police were able to find out something. It's also possible that when the girl has time to think it over, she may come back of her own free will. It's been our experience here on Hot Line—and the police would tell you the same thing—that this happens as often as not."

The woman, hanging up, seemed a little comforted.

It turned out to be a quieter night than most. Which was just another small example of the perversity of life, Rachel reflected. She would rather it was a busy night, the phone ringing steadily, keeping her mind off Luke and the story of his brief affair with Amy Gardner that she wished she hadn't heard and that he himself had probably regretted telling ever since.

Most of all, Rachel was troubled by the sudden suspicion that had flared up after he left Saturday night and that kept recurring at odd moments no matter how hard she tried to quell it.

As now, for instance, with time on her hands, she suddenly found herself thinking that money needn't have been Luke's only motive. It might have been added to something else, something to do with that long-ago affair. There was Amy feeling neglected, lonely, thinking of Luke, perhaps, and the way she had once felt toward him. She had called him one night not too far back and spoken with some bitterness to Rachel about his lack of interest in her. What if she had called him again the night of her death insisting that he come and see her? And when he came, well—what?

What indeed? Rachel frowned impatiently over the way she was letting her imagination run away with her.

She forced her thoughts in another direction, Luke's interview with Captain Betz that afternoon. She had half expected him to stop by when he left the police station but she hadn't heard from him; not today, not since Saturday.

Maybe he felt a little embarrassed over having told her about his affair with Amy. Maybe he intended to avoid her for a while.

She frowned again. All these maybes—they had no more substance than the wisps of fog drifting around the street light outside the front window.

Why didn't someone call? That was part of her problem, the silent phone, the silent office. An old building like this, deserted most nights, was enough to give anyone weird thoughts.

The phone rang. She snatched it up. "Hot Line, this is Martha. Can I help you?"

It was a young girl's voice saying diffidently, "I don't know if what's bothering me is anything important enough for you to help with—I thought I'd ask, though—"

"Yes?" Rachel said encouragingly.

"There's this boy, you see. He's a senior, he's really a wheel at school and he's asked me to go to the spring dance with him but I don't have anything to wear—a formal, I mean—and my mother said she couldn't afford to buy me one so I couldn't go. I've just been wondering if Hot Line —if you ever help with things like that? I mean, like I wear size eight and if people ever give you clothes they don't need—you know, something pretty—they probably don't but I thought well, nothing to lose by asking . . ." the girl's voice trailed off into dispirited silence.

Rachel was at a loss. She had never been asked anything like this before or heard it mentioned by any of the other aides. A Salvation Army referral? Did people give formals nice enough for a spring dance at the high school to the Salvation Army? That young voice, though, unexpectant but at the same time hopeful of a miracle—a wheel had asked her, she needed something really nice to wear—size eight—

No use making a lightning-quick review of her own wardrobe. She wore size ten or sometimes eleven herself—or could it be altered? Not to look right probably. But what about other Hot Line aides?

"When is the dance?" she asked.

"A week from this Friday."

"Well, we don't handle clothes here," Rachel said, "but I just thought of something that might work. I could post a notice on our bulletin board asking if any of the other aides has a size eight formal they could let you have or knows of anyone else who has one suitable for your dance."

"Oh, would you do that? Shall I give you my name and phone number so you can let me know?"

"Let's do it another way—you call me back."

"All right. How soon? I told the boy I'd let him know for

sure by the end of this week. If I can't go, he has to have time to ask someone else, you see."

Rachel saw. The girl was rushing her but the boy couldn't very well ask someone else at the last minute.

"Well, call me Friday night," she said. "I'll put the notice up right away and we'll see what happens."

"Oh, thank you so much. I'll call you."

Rachel used a magic marker to print the notice in large letters and thumbtacked it to the bulletin board.

The girl's request had made a little stir that took her out of herself. But when the notice was tacked up the silence settled around her again.

She looked at her watch. Only five after ten. Nearly two hours to go yet.

She had brought along a book she had taken out of the library that day but she couldn't settle down with it. She laid it aside to wander around the room.

The phone brought her back to the desk. A boy's voice said, "Hey, Martha, don't you know your horse just got loose? You don't want a car to hit him, do you?"

"Of course not," Rachel answered playing it straight. "I'll go out and catch him right now and ride him back to pasture."

Giggles in the background. The call cheered her up as she filled out a daily sheet writing "Joke call" under category and adding it to the slim sheaf on the desk.

Presently she went out into the kitchen and made herself a cup of coffee. Had the fog cleared away yet? All she could see in the back window was the reflection of the bright ceiling light. She turned it off and went over to the window to peer out.

As her eyes adjusted to the dark she saw that the post light near the corner of the building, the only light in the parking lot, was haloed by a fine mist, not quite rain. The weather hadn't changed since she drove downtown.

The parking lot was deserted except for her car. But as

she stood there drinking her coffee, she caught sight of something that moved, a darker shadow near her car blending into the tall yew hedge off to her left, the boundary line on that side of the parking lot. Wind stirring a branch?

But there was no wind. The night was very still under an opaque sky.

Someone was out there.

Her car, she thought instantly. Someone trying to steal it. No, not her car. The shadow moved away from it toward the back porch.

Could she be seen herself silhouetted against the light that shone in from the front room?

She moved back a step and went on watching, a little frightened but curious, too, as to what anyone, not after her car, could be doing out there at that hour of the night.

The shadow resolved itself into a man's figure barely glimpsed and then lost to sight moving close to the back porch. Straining to see, Rachel caught another glimpse of the figure vanishing around the corner of the building onto the driveway.

She ran into the front room turning off the desk lamp on the way. But when she drew back the curtain there was no one visible on the street outside. Just a car going by and the deep black of a maple tree close by.

Whoever had been in the parking lot must have turned in the other direction hugging the front of the building next door.

The phone put an end to her vigil. She turned the desk lamp back on and picked up the receiver.

It was a woman, separated from her husband, who wasn't keeping up support payments for her and their children.

While she poured out her troubles at some length, Rachel thought she heard a sound in the hall, as of someone moving very quietly trying to make no sound at all.

She stiffened in her chair, suddenly realizing that it had

been only an assumption on her part that the man out in back had gone away.

". . . So I told the bum to get out and he packed his things and left," the woman was saying. "But now he hardly gives us enough money to put food on the table. And the light company's called wanting their bill paid . . ."

Wasn't that a board creaking out in the hall, perhaps on the stairs?

Rachel couldn't be sure with the woman's voice droning in her ear. Asking a question, actually.

"He can't get away with not supporting us, can he? I called him at work yesterday and said he'd better have a check in the mail by today but he didn't send one. I've been sitting here by myself worrying about it ever since I put the kids to bed. There's some way to make him support us, isn't there?"

Wasn't that a different sound, the faint click of a door closing softly? The outside door it would have to be, if any.

Rachel's hand shook slightly reaching for the file. "The Legal Aid Society will be able to tell you just what your rights are if you call them tomorrow," she said. "Would you like to have their phone number?"

"The Legal Aid Society? Maybe I've heard of them. What is their number?"

Rachel gave it to her, the woman wrote it down and at last hung up.

Once again Rachel turned off the desk lamp, went to the window and drew back the curtain. Once again there was no one visible outside. And no sound now in the hall.

Could she have imagined that someone was out there? There were often creaks in the old building at night.

But she hadn't imagined the shadowy figure moving around in the parking lot.

She remembered then that she hadn't made out a daily sheet on the woman who had just called. She looked at the clock. Ten of eleven now. The woman had been on the phone a good ten minutes.

Rachel's thoughts returned to the man outside as she added the sheet to the others.

Call the police about him? Yes. She had no guarantee that he was gone.

She dialed the police station.

She was back on the phone when the cruiser turned in onto the driveway a few minutes later. By the time she was free to look out the kitchen window the officer, still sweeping the area with his flashlight, was heading for the front door.

Rachel met him in the hall. "Nobody out there now, ma'am," he reported. "Few twigs of evergreen on the ground that might be from someone standing against the hedge. Nothing else, though."

She waited while he went upstairs to look around.

"No sign of anyone up there," he said when he came down.

"He may not have been inside at all but I definitely saw him out in the parking lot," Rachel said.

"Well, we'll keep an eye on the place. Anything worries you, just call us again, ma'am."

Rachel thanked him and went back inside, double-locking the door.

The thought struck her as the cruiser left that this was the police routine Amy Gardner had become familiar with through her calls about a prowler.

A prowler. The man she had seen was one.

A chill touched her spine.

When Susan Crowe arrived at midnight Rachel told her there had been a man outside who might or might not have come into the building.

"Some drunk probably," Susan said taking it in stride. "Nothing around here worth the trouble to steal. I'll watch, though, while you go out to your car. Lock the doors when you get in it."

There was no one in sight, nothing to be afraid of when Rachel went out to the parking lot. Susan waved to her from the kitchen window as she drove away.

The parking lot at her apartment house was well lighted and there was the reinforcement of a couple who lived on the first floor turning into it ahead of her. She walked inside with them, pleased to have their company; and even more pleased to lock and bolt her own door behind her.

Tomorrow she would call Mrs. Holt and tell her there had been a prowler out in back tonight.

A prowler, not a drunk as Susan had suggested, moving too carefully to be one.

She couldn't imagine what he wanted outside or inside the building. If he really had come inside. She still wasn't too sure about that.

CHAPTER SIXTEEN

Rachel wasn't able to reach Mrs. Holt until late the next morning. Not long after she had talked with her Captain Betz called. He had just received a report on her call the night before and wanted to hear her version of it at first-hand.

Repeating it by daylight with the sun streaming in the window it seemed to have less substance. She was even less sure that whoever had been outside had entered the building and gone upstairs.

"I was already a bit nervous from having seen the man outside," she explained when she came to that part of her story. "And there was also a woman on the phone who was taking up most of my attention. The creakings I heard could have been the old house settling the way it does sometimes. But the man outside was real. Just a figure, of course, but fairly tall. He came close to the back porch. It was to keep out of sight, I thought, if he'd seen me at the window with the light behind me coming from the other room."

Betz absorbed this in silence for a moment and then asked, "Anyone ever been known to hang around out there before?"

"No. When I told the director about it just before you called, she said this was the first time anything like that had happened in the three years Hot Line has had its office in the building. She's going to speak to the owner about additional lights in the parking lot. And also about a new lock on the front door with all the tenants having keys to it so that no one else will have access at night."

"It should have been done long ago just on general principles," Betz said. "It's never a good idea that anyone can go in and out of a building even if the tenants keep their own offices locked. It makes it worse that there's someone alone there in the Hot Line office all night."

"Yes, but there's never been any problem before," Rachel pointed out. "It's just an old run-down house that would have no attraction for a thief."

"We don't know who the man outside was or what he wanted," Betz said. "It's quite a coincidence that not only is it the first time anything like that ever happened around there but that you were on duty when it did."

"I've thought of that too," Rachel said. "But I don't see how it could have any connection with Mrs. Gardner's murder, Captain. If she was killed by the prowler and the prowler read what I told you in the paper there'd still be no way for him to tie it in with Hot Line. That information never came out."

"No, not officially, Mrs. Carey, but there are always leaks. Mrs. Gardner's family, for one instance, knows that you got connected with the case through Hot Line. Who's to say they haven't mentioned it to anyone?"

"So that it might have got back to the prowler that way? Seems farfetched to me."

"Oh, the prowler . . ." Betz threw the words away but his tone picked up forcefulness as he added, "I think you should be careful, Mrs. Carey, about going to the Hot Line office. Better yet, stop going for a while."

"I couldn't just stop. Not without giving a couple of weeks' notice. It's hard enough as it is to keep the schedule filled twenty-four hours a day, seven days a week."

"Well, at least take precautions going in and out of the building. Make sure one of the other aides keeps an eye on you."

"Yes, I can arrange for that going home. And it's still daylight now when I get there." Rachel hesitated and then said,

"I can't imagine, though, how I could give anyone cause to
worry. I've already told everything I knew from my conversations with Amy Gardner."

"Not quite everything," Betz reminded her. "She mentioned something you couldn't remember the night she was
killed. Something she was doing or going to do before she
went outside."

"Oh . . . Oh yes. I'm sorry, I'd forgotten all about it. It's
gone completely now anyway, I guess."

"Well, try to remember it. It might not be anything important but then again it might be."

"I'll try," Rachel said.

She gave it some thought while she was fixing lunch for
herself. But she didn't concentrate on it long. She was more
inclined to mull over what Captain Betz had said. She must
be careful was what stood out. In some way the prowler
who had killed Amy Gardner might still be concerned over
things the dead girl had talked to her about.

Except, she thought next, that the prowler didn't seem to
loom too large in Betz's calculations, his tone almost dismissing him, emphasizing instead the family's knowledge of
Amy's Hot Line calls to Rachel.

That didn't make much sense, though. Paul Gardner and
Luke knew all there was to know about her conversations
with Rachel and one or the other would have passed on the
information to Franklin Lambert. So why should any of
them still be concerned about her role in the case?

But Captain Betz was. So was Celia.

Sergeant Morris returned from his second trip to Prince
William Community College right after Betz's call to Rachel
and reported to the captain immediately. Betz had first sent
him there nearly two weeks ago to verify Paul Gardner's
statement that he had been in the college library the night
of his wife's murder from around nine o'clock when his last
class ended until ten o'clock when the library closed.

Morris's first inquiry had ended in frustration. The assistant librarian in charge that night had left on a Caribbean cruise the Friday after Amy Gardner's death, Morris was told, and wouldn't be back for another ten days. Her student helpers either didn't know Paul Gardner at all or hadn't noticed what time he was in the library that night.

But the assistant librarian, now back from her vacation, was able to answer Morris's questions. She was on friendly terms with Mr. Gardner, she said, and he had stopped at her desk when he came into the library that night soon after nine o'clock. Some remark he made brought up a quotation he attributed to Zola but she thought was from something Anatole France had written. She told him she would look it up when she found the time and he went on to the English Literature section. She saw him at the shelves and a little later sitting at a table. Someone else stopped at her desk just then and after that she went to the reference room to look up the quotation. It was close to nine-thirty by that time and when she got back to her desk Mr. Gardner was gone. He did not return before ten o'clock closing time.

Sergeant Morris relayed all this to Betz.

"Let's take a look at that statement of his again," the latter said.

But as Morris started to get it out of the file, a great commotion began in the lobby with a woman screeching at the top of her lungs and a man shouting back at the top of his; other voices, trying to quiet them down, were lost in the cacophony.

"What the hell—?" said Betz. "Go see what's going on out there, will you, Morris?"

Morris was gone for several minutes during which the uproar gradually died down.

He came back laughing. "Husband-and-wife fracas," he said. "She's had him arrested for assault but she's lucky he didn't kill her. Seems she thought he was cheating on her and to get back at him she took a pair of scissors and cut his entire wardrobe to pieces, including a new hundred-and-fifty-dollar suit he just bought last week. The crowning touch is, as they're beginning to get it sorted out, that he wasn't cheating on her at all."

"Jesus," said Betz. "It would have been justifiable homicide."

Morris went back to the file, got out Paul Gardner's statement and glanced through it. "Here we are." He read aloud, "'I went to the library at nine o'clock when my last class was over to check on some material I wanted. I left for home around the time the library closed, arriving shortly after ten-thirty. I am not sure of the exact time on that. I drove into the carport, went in the house by the back door and—'"

Morris broke off. "That's it," he said.

"Smart," Betz commented. "Not an out-and-out lie—he doesn't say he was in the library until it closed—just that he left for home around the time it did."

Morris pondered half to himself, "So now we know he had twice as much time as we thought to get home and get into a fight with Mrs. Gardner—or pick up one where they left off earlier—that ended in her murder."

"More likely picking one up where they left off," Betz commented. "According to Mrs. Carey, she was uptight when she called her that night, out to show her husband she could handle her problems herself." He grinned suddenly. "With or without scissors to cut up his clothes."

The next moment he was serious again. "You'd better have a talk with him right away," he said, reaching for his phone. "I'll see if he's home."

Paul Gardner was but said he had a two o'clock class.

"Well, this is a small matter that shouldn't take up too much of your time," Betz replied. "Sergeant Morris will be right out."

When Morris arrived he pulled in behind the car he knew was Amy Gardner's parked beside her husband's in the double carport.

Paul Gardner was outside on the patio and came around

the rambling one-story house to greet Morris. He wore a turtleneck jersey, sport jacket and slacks, apparently ready to leave for the college.

He led the way back to the patio, pulled a chair forward and said, "Sit down, Sergeant."

"Thank you." Morris sat down opposite him and began, "Just a couple more questions, sir, in connection with the statement you gave us about the night your wife was killed. You went to the library, you said, right after your last class."

"Yes." Behind his dark-rimmed glasses Paul Gardner's gray-blue eyes took on alertness.

"And you were at the library, sir, from nine till around closing time?"

But even as he spoke Morris realized that the other wasn't going to fall into that trap. The very fact that he asked the question conveyed its own warning.

"I don't believe I put the exact time I left the library in my statement," Paul Gardner replied. "I couldn't have said I stayed there until it closed because I didn't. I left around nine-thirty or thereabouts—I didn't look at my watch—and went out to my car. I didn't start home right away, though. I sat there and had a cigarette. There were a few things I wanted to think over and it seemed a good time for it, nice and quiet in the parking area, no one else around."

"How long did you stay there, Mr. Gardner?"

"Well, when people started coming out of the building and lights were being put out, I knew it was around closing time and left and came home."

"You just sat there for half an hour?"

"I doubt it was that long. But as I've said, I wasn't clocking it. I'd guess, though, that it was twenty to twenty-five minutes."

So there it was, thought Morris. He had avoided the trap or, possibly, was telling the simple truth. "That's a lot of time to sit," he said. "Like the other day when I waited ten minutes for someone it seemed more like an hour."

"Not when you have things on your mind," Paul Gardner replied briefly.

What things—killing a wife who was a drag on you and inheriting a lot of money from her?

Sergeant Morris could hardly ask that question. Not yet, at least, with nothing to back it up.

About all they had so far, he reflected, driving back to the police station, was motive. Well, opportunity, too, even if he was telling the truth about sitting outside the library for nearly half an hour. There would still be a few minutes' leeway for him to act.

The weapon was no kind of evidence, a heavy doorstop, wiped clean of fingerprints. It was a weapon that made it look like an impulse murder.

"So that's that," he reported back to Betz. "Unless—or until—we get something more on him. I don't know what, though, that's for sure."

"God, this case," Betz brooded aloud. "When we had hopes of the prowler we got the Jackson kid. Then with the jewelry we got Corley, who's now got that lawyer hollering that we've got no case. Which we probably haven't. Because Corley's story, the more you think of it, is just screwy enough to be true."

Betz sighed morosely. "Gardner's my favorite—the husband always is—but there's Welford too. All that smooth talk of his when he was here yesterday about working on an advertising layout that whole evening didn't impress me one bit. He was alone in his apartment so it's no alibi at all. Lambert's the only one of the three who has one . . ."

Betz paused glancing at Morris who was listening with respectful attention. "Maybe you ought to check Lambert's alibi again and have another talk with him. After that there's Welford. Beginning with Lambert, we've got to start reaching out."

"Yessir," said Morris. "Will tomorrow do? I've got to interrogate those witnesses this afternoon on the Mansfield robbery."

"Tomorrow then."

"Tomorrow afternoon, sir? I'm due in court tomorrow morning and it will probably take up most of the day. That rape case on Wolcott Street that gave us so much trouble."

"Afternoon's fine." Betz's tone was curt with annoyance directed at himself over not having his subordinates' assignments at his fingertips. There were, after all, only six of them in the investigative division. Trouble was, he reflected, he had the Gardner case on his mind too much. Just because it was out of the usual run was no reason for him to get out of touch with their regular work load.

As he left the captain's office Morris found himself wondering if they were ever going to solve the Gardner murder. Every time they thought they were getting somewhere with it, it fell apart in their hands. Like cobwebs . . .

CHAPTER SEVENTEEN

If Paul Gardner had followed his inclination he would have nodded to Miss Koch, the assistant librarian, and walked right on when he encountered her in the hall outside the college library late that Wednesday afternoon. He had known she was back from vacation and had realized as soon as Sergeant Morris asked what time he had left the library the night of Amy's murder that Miss Koch was behind it.

He hadn't given her a thought since that night; least of all that she had noticed his comings and goings; or that the police would be checking with her right after she returned from her trip.

No point in feeling resentment toward Miss Koch, though. She had only been doing her duty as a responsible citizen, relating what she had observed of his activities that night and thereby adding another black mark against him with the police.

At least he could be thankful he had merely glided over that half-hour time gap. If he had said he had been in the library until closing time he would now be in serious trouble.

So he stopped in the hall and said cordially, "Miss Koch. Good to have you back. How was your vacation?"

Her face turned pink. From guilt over what she had told the police, he thought, having no idea that the sedate spinster in her mid-thirties had long cherished a secret crush on him.

"It was very nice, thank you," she replied and went on

quickly, "I'm so sorry about what happened to your wife, Mr. Gardner."

"Thank you."

"A terrible thing. It must have been a great shock to you."

"Yes, it certainly was." He gave her a polite nod and went on down the hall.

Miss Koch's gaze followed him wistfully. Her interview with Sergeant Morris that morning was farthest from her mind since she had taken at face value his assurance that it was a matter of routine. Mr. Gardner, so attractive, so pleasant, always ready to exchange a few words with her, couldn't possibly be under suspicion.

And now he was a widower. Not right to think of that. Untimely. But still . . .

Miss Koch, going about her affairs, allowed herself to dream a little.

Paul Gardner, driving home from the college, dwelt on the fact that his marriage to Amy had been doomed to failure from the start.

His fault or hers? God only knew.

Well, no, he knew himself that they were both at fault.

That dependency on her mother should have warned him off from the start. He had sensed some of its intricacies of love and resentment and jealousy but only the tip of the iceberg, he realized when it was too late, with the tortuous submerged rest brought to the surface by her mother's death.

Before that he had been amused and a little flattered by Amy's childlike readiness to consult and defer to him. He had found it challenging to overcome the perverse moody streak she revealed every now and then. A little fey, a little elusive when she set out to be charming, she had sometimes caught him off balance but he had always felt equal to coping with her.

Christ, how fatuous he had been! He should have known better from the start; and above all, he should have run a

mile when he saw how she acted after her mother's death.
But he had let her need of him prevent it.

And then he had failed her. Just by trying to establish a
normal life style, keep up with his job—and since last fall
escape from her into teaching two nights a week—he had
failed her, made her feel so rejected that she had been reduced to calling Hot Line, pouring out her troubles to
Rachel Carey.

Who wasn't herself too much older than Amy—four or
five years?—but as different from her as day from night in
maturity, a sense of balance that kept her doing something
useful, while in the middle of getting a divorce, instead of
sitting home like Amy feeling sorry for herself.

Who was at fault in Rachel Carey's divorce?

That was a pointless question because in the end, as in
his own situation, wasn't it everyone's fault? Parents, grand-
parents, how far back did you go before you could pinpoint
blame for how people's marriages turned out?

There was no answer to that.

What had Amy found to say about him all those times she
had called Rachel Carey?

This question still lingered in his mind when he arrived
home.

He went from room to room in his quiet empty house
unable to settle anywhere and finally found himself at the
kitchen phone looking up and dialing Rachel's number, his
eyes turned away from the spot where Amy had lain dead
on the floor.

If Rachel Carey wasn't home it was doubtful if he would
ever call her again, he thought, as her phone began to ring.
Probably not. Probably he would let sleeping dogs lie in
spite of wanting to know more about those calls from Amy.

Rachel answered on the fourth ring.

"Mrs. Carey?" he said.

"Yes."

"Paul Gardner. Would it be all right if I came to see you?

When I talked with you before I mentioned, you may remember, that there were some questions I'd like to ask about Amy's calls to you."

"Yes, I remember. I'll be glad to answer any that I can."

"Are you free this evening if I stop by around eight?"

"Yes, I'll be here."

"Thanks very much, I'll see you then."

Straight to the point, Rachel thought as they both hung up. Abrupt really, as if he had too much on his mind for the amenities of small talk.

And yet what was there that she could tell him about Amy's calls that he didn't already know? Well, if there was anything at all, it would remove the least doubt that she had told the whole story.

The phone rang again. It was her father-in-law asking her to dinner the next night. "I hope you're free," he said. "Griff went down to Creighton's Dock this afternoon and came back with some beautiful crabs fresh from the bay. You know how good they'll be, the way he fixes them."

"Indeed I do," Rachel said having enjoyed many meals cooked by Griffin, her father-in-law's houseman for more years than either of them cared to remember. "Love to come," she added. "What time?"

"Well, if you get here a little after six we'll have plenty of time for a drink or two and then dinner. Don't want it to be late for you, driving back alone from the country."

"You make me feel nice and pampered," Rachel said.

"Good. That's what I want to do."

Once again he was trying to make up for the fact that Neil, his son, had not pampered her at all. Rachel felt uncomfortable over it and changed the subject by telling him about Paul Gardner's impending visit.

"Gardner?" He spoke on a disapproving note. "I thought you were well out of that unfortunate affair by this time. Instead, you're letting the man come to your apartment. I don't like the idea, Rachel."

"But if you knew him—I just can't imagine that he killed his wife."

"Can't you? I reckon the police don't have that problem. He must be high on their list of suspects."

"I suppose you're right," Rachel conceded. "I could have made some excuse." She hadn't wanted to, she realized, but could hardly tell her father-in-law that.

"Look," she continued, "will it make you feel better if I mention that you know he's visiting me the minute he comes in the door?"

"Yes indeed. Just be careful, hear?"

"I will. See you tomorrow evening around six."

After she hung up Rachel discovered that her father-in-law's comments had turned her thoughts back to last night's prowler. Paul Gardner? As a murder suspect, couldn't he have been that shadowy figure?

She didn't find it possible to regard him in that light.

She found it even less possible when he arrived that night, apologetic over intruding on her. Far from considering him a threat, his constraint made her want to put him at ease, supplying him with a drink and getting him settled in a chair facing hers.

They talked about the weather, how unseasonably warm it had been today and that tomorrow was supposed to be much the same.

Rachel went on to ask if he was now back on his regular teaching schedule.

Oh yes, he replied, back in his routine, evening classes twice a week and a varied daytime program.

"We both know, of course," he appended, taking advantage of the opening she had given him, "that the evening classes were a major grievance of Amy's."

"Yes, but I got the impression that she couldn't help herself," Rachel said. "That it began with her mother's death."

Paul Gardner shook his head. "Much earlier than that from what her psychiatrist, the second one, that is, told me.

He felt it went all the way back to earliest childhood, to the first time she found out she could get her own way by making a big fuss. He said I had to be patient and wait for her to work out a new life style, behavior pattern, whatever you want to call it. That was easier said than done. Things got pretty rough between us at times."

"They were bound to I suppose," Rachel said feeling that some comment was necessary.

He took a swallow of his drink and continued, "What I can't get over, Mrs. Carey, is her calls to you. I know it's an imposition but I wish you'd try to remember as much as you can of what she said about herself and me and our marriage."

"Well . . ." With his gaze fixed on her, Rachel tried, as she had with Captain Betz, to recall details of her conversations with Amy Gardner. But two weeks had passed since the first attempt and she found it harder still to bring them back to mind.

By the time she reached the last conversation of all Paul Gardner was on his feet walking back and forth across the room.

"God, that trap for the prowler," he said at the end, returning to his chair. "No thought of danger, nothing beyond the idea that she wanted to catch him."

"I should have tried harder to stop her."

"She wouldn't have listened, not in the mood she was in when I left that night. You were right in assuming that we'd just had an argument. It began in a small way and then— you know how these things do?—blew up into a real fight."

He got back to his feet to pace the floor again. "She was right, too, that I rejected her," he said, a remorseful note in his voice. "I got so fed up with the way she kept talking about everything that ever happened to her and taking her emotional pulse all the time."

He had finished his drink. Rachel picked up both their glasses and said, "I'll make us another."

"Let me help." He followed her out to the kitchen.

She was conscious of his nearness within its narrow confines but not with any sense of uneasiness. Rather, she felt drawn to him, wanting to find some words of comfort for the way he seemed to blame himself for what had happened, even though she had softened, in her account of her last conversation with Amy, the brittle anger and defiance the dead girl had revealed toward him.

He didn't help with the drinks; just stood there looking at Rachel, tension turned inward showing on his face.

He took his glass from Rachel and burst out, "From what you've told me I realize now how much she really needed sympathy calling Hot Line. A hell of a way for a marriage to turn out, isn't it? The truth is, I wanted to back out of marrying her at all, when I saw how she acted after her mother died. But the way she turned to me, there was no decent way to back out then."

And Paul Gardner was a decent man, Rachel thought, suddenly wanting to smooth back the lock of hair he pushed at so nervously.

Startled and ashamed of the impulse with Amy so recently, brutally dead, she collected herself and said, "Let's go back in the living room."

The phone rang just as they sat down. Rachel excused herself and went into her bedroom where she could answer it with more privacy than the kitchen phone offered.

It was Luke Welford. "I hope it's not too late to drive down to see you tonight," he said.

"It certainly is." She looked at her watch. "Almost nine-thirty. Besides, there's someone here."

"Oh. Male or female?"

"What a question . . . How'd it go yesterday at the police station? At least Betz didn't lock you up."

"No, but he didn't give me any gold star either."

"You didn't expect him to, did you?" Rachel countered. "He hasn't even caught the prowler yet or anyone else, far as I know." Then, thinking of the shadowy figure outside the Hot Line office the night before, she couldn't keep herself from adding, "How late did Betz keep you?"

"Till almost six o'clock. Worked overtime himself, you see. Wonder if he gets paid for it."

"I have no idea. But look, I mustn't keep talking when I have company."

"See you tomorrow night?"

"Oh, I'm afraid I can't. I'm having dinner with my father-in-law."

"And Friday night's Hot Line?"

"Yes."

"Which means you'll be sitting in that office—wherever it is—until midnight?"

"That's right . . ." Rachel spoke in a faraway tone, absorbing the implications of Luke's casual wherever it is. He didn't know where the Hot Line office was. She had never told him; or Paul Gardner; or, for that matter, anyone. She wasn't supposed to.

Whoever had been there last night couldn't have had anything to do with the murder; must have been, in fact, some casual prowler.

The relief she felt made her realize how much unacknowledged anxiety the incident had been causing her.

She brought her attention back to Luke who was asking her to go out Saturday night.

"That's fine with me."

"Okay, pick you up around eight?"

"Yes, see you then."

Funny, Rachel thought as she hung up, that Captain Betz hadn't caught that point either, talking with her this morning. Because they both knew where the Hot Line office was, they had overlooked the fact that it wasn't general knowledge. Not a state secret exactly, but not all that easy to find out.

She felt better about Luke and about Paul Gardner too.

It was a little upsetting, though, playing mother confessor to both of them in their ambivalent relationships with Amy Gardner. First her cousin last weekend and now her husband.

But at least neither of them would ever know about the outpourings of the other.

And it had all come about through Hot Line.

Quirk of fate—or something, she thought, shrugging it off as she returned to the living room.

Paul Gardner stood up when she appeared. "It's safe to come back now, Mrs. Carey," he said on a rueful note. "No more dumping of private woes on you."

She smiled. "Don't worry about it. We all need to do it sometimes." She paused. "Except that it's usually done on a first-name basis. You know, like Rachel—Paul?"

He laughed. "That does sound better. But look, you hadn't even touched your drink when you got that phone call. I saved mine to have it with you."

Conversation flowed easily after that, Amy not mentioned while they had their drinks. He asked Rachel how long she had been working at Hot Line and what kinds of things she had to handle.

She gave him a brief outline of the purpose of the organization and then, recalling the inquiry she had received last night that didn't touch on a major problem, she added, "There's always something new. Last night, for instance, a girl wanted to know if I could help her get a size eight evening dress for a high school dance. Best I could do was put up a notice on our bulletin board."

"Size eight," Paul Gardner mused. "That's small, isn't it?"

"Yes. I'm a ten or eleven myself."

"I think that was Amy's size. And she left a closetful of dresses that I'll have to do something with—"

"Oh, but that's not the sort of thing—"

"I know. But couldn't you just pick one out for the girl, Mrs.—uh—Rachel? Amy," a slight hesitancy, "had good taste —her mother saw to that—and had quite a few nice party dresses. I'm sure it would please her if the girl had one of them."

"Well . . ." Rachel looked doubtful for a moment but then remembering the girl's need, the rapture she would feel over the kind of expensive dress Amy Gardner would have had, she put aside her doubts and said, "That would be wonderful."

"All right, when would it be convenient for you to come pick one out? I'll be away tomorrow but any other day is fine."

The girl was to call Rachel Friday night. It was settled that Rachel would go to his house around five o'clock Friday afternoon when he would be home from the college.

Presently she heard herself ask, "What was Mrs. Lambert like, Paul?"

His answer came without need for reflection. "Charming, fascinating, men still falling for her in her forties," he said. "As they had been, apparently, all her life. In an earlier age she would have been called a great beauty. Rather a spoiled beauty, too, I might add. Used to being the center of attention wherever she went."

"The Victorian Age. The Edwardian Age. It must have been marvelous to be a great beauty in those days. Think of all the homage . . ."

"It still goes on. Mrs. Lambert got plenty of it."

"Amy said the same things about her," Rachel continued. "It was a disadvantage to her, though, having a mother who was a great beauty."

"Oh yes, put her in the shade. But Amy never gave up trying to compete with her. Sometimes it seemed to me they were both in competition with each other." He shook his head. "They really had a peculiar relationship. For example, one night not long before her mother's death, Amy wanted her to . . ."

And so they were back on Amy Gardner.

To whom all roads led.

CHAPTER EIGHTEEN

"He was here the whole evening," the bartender said, buttoning himself into a snowy white jacket that set off the glowing brown of his face. "Had a drink with Mr. Woods—you know, the city manager?—before this dinner they was having began."

The bartender paused for thought. "Next time I sees him was oh, maybe about half-past eight. They'd finished their dinner by then—I could see the head table right through the doorway there—" a wave of his hand indicated the open archway between the cocktail lounge and the long, finely proportioned dining room of Lafayette Inn, "and the speaker, he was being introduced by the head of that committee they got for fixing up downtown. Mr. Lambert, he went out into the hall—reckon he was going to the men's room—and stopped at the bar on his way back and said, 'William, I'll have me a quick one.' I knew he meant bourbon on the rocks and I fixed it for him. He tossed it down real quick and went on to the dining room, slipping in quiet, you know, not to draw notice with the speaker just getting started."

It was close to five o'clock the next afternoon, the cocktail lounge still deserted but William moving back and forth as he talked, getting ready for patrons who would soon be coming in.

Sergeant Morris strolled over to the archway and looked into the dining room, the tables set for dinner, silver and glassware gleaming, tablecloths the same soft shade of green as the brocaded draperies at the tall windows.

There was no dinner meeting tonight. When there was, the head table, consisting of several smaller tables pushed together, was set up at the far end of the room, convenient to the kitchen.

On Morris's left was a semi-enclosed cloakroom with a door in the outer wall that led into the hall.

That was all there was to see. He turned back to the bartender, asking, "What time did the meeting end?"

"Oh, 'long about half-past nine, quarter of ten. Most people left right away—there was quite a lot at the dinner—but some come in here for a drink."

"And Mr. Lambert was one of them."

The bartender's teeth flashed in a grin. "Indeed he was, sir, right up till the time I left. I generally leaves earlier—John, the other bartender, comes on at five and he stays till closing—but when there's doings like that night, I stays later. Reckon I was here another hour before things quieted down. Mr. Lambert was sitting right over there," William pointed to a window table, "having drinks with three or four men that was at the meeting with him."

"So he was here until at least ten-thirty?"

"Yes indeed, sir. Later than that 'cause I brought another round of drinks to his table just before I left."

"Do you remember who was sitting with him?"

William reeled off names promptly. Morris recognized two of them, both upstanding citizens.

That was that, he reflected as he thanked William and left. The bartender, a fixture at Lafayette Inn, an upstanding citizen himself, had given Lambert a firm alibi. So firm that there was little point in tracking down the long list of waiters who had served at the dinner to verify it.

Little point either, Morris thought, in going to see Lambert. Still, he'd go. Betz was a stickler for thoroughness and with pay raises for the police department approved by city council in the new budget, it was a good time to be on his toes.

Morris didn't go out through the lobby. He turned the other way into the hall next to the dining room and went out a side door to the parking lot, thinking about his raise on the way and about getting a new car. Not an extravagance considering that the one he had was almost seven years old, a present from his parents when he finished college. And it wasn't as if he were a married man like most of his colleagues. Not even engaged although it was possible he might be—would be, if Nancy had her way—within the next few months.

He wasn't so sure about it himself. Plenty of time yet to get married.

He had called Lambert at his office earlier. Lambert was on his way out but said Morris could catch him at home around five o'clock if he wanted to stop by then.

Morris arrived a few minutes after five. The house was impressive for sheer size, not for its Victorian design, he thought, turning in at the driveway. Gray with white shutters, it stood on a rise, surrounded by acres of lawn. It looked beautiful at that time of year with azaleas of every color, dogwood, flowering peach and crab coming into bloom, set off by the lush green of newly cut grass. In the back of the house, screened by it from the street, was a fenced-in swimming pool.

Lambert was getting out of his car in the garage when Morris braked to a stop close by. He walked over to greet him with a smile and a handshake. "Come right in, Sergeant —uh—?"

"Morris."

"Oh yes. Slipped my mind for a moment. We met before, didn't we, right after," his smile faded, "my stepdaughter's death?"

Morris nodded and followed him around to the front door, Lambert explaining, "When I'm alone I go in the back way but Ruby, who looks after me, doesn't like people tramping through her kitchen. By myself, it's just walking through but if I dare bring anyone in with me, it turns into tramping through."

Morris laughed, inclined to like Franklin Lambert, genial, outgoing, quick to put him at his ease. His job, dealing with all sorts of people and their conflicting views, gave him plenty of practice in that, of course.

He led the way into the front hall, larger than the living room in Morris's apartment, past spacious, handsomely furnished rooms on either side to a small room in back equipped as an office with a desk and bookshelves filled with volumes on urban affairs.

"Drink, Sergeant?" he inquired going over to a cabinet that opened out into a bar. "Or don't you drink on duty?"

"No, I don't, sir. I'd like a Coke, though."

Lambert made himself a stiff bourbon on the rocks, poured Morris a Coke and sat down in the leather swivel chair at his desk, gesturing Morris into a comfortable leather armchair opposite him.

"So what can I do for you, Sergeant?" he inquired taking a good healthy swallow from his glass.

Nothing really, Morris thought, considering the alibi supplied by William at the inn.

But he had to go through the motions and began, "Well, it just seems like a good idea, sir, to check back with the people closest to Mrs. Gardner now that they've had a little time to get over the shock of her death. You know, in case some little thing comes to mind that might help."

"I see." Lambert drained his glass, slightly prominent hazel eyes resting on Morris thoughtfully. He was a good-looking man, the latter reflected, studying him. Athletic build, took care of himself. Must be in his forties or getting there but didn't show it. Well dressed too. His checked jacket alone must have cost what would be a week's pay for Morris.

"Paul told me you went to see him yesterday," Lambert said next. "You were trying to nail him down, he said, on the odd half hour before he got home the night of Amy's death. Seems like you're at a dead end, Sergeant. Paul had plenty to put up with but he'd never have killed her. Never in this world. A divorce, yes, it might well have come to that. But kill her? No indeed."

"Well, I'm not sure I'd be that ready to vouch for anyone myself, sir," Morris said. "When they were under stress, I mean."

"Most cases I'd agree but I feel safe vouching for Paul. That's how much I think of him. He's a fine dependable fellow, not running away from what he got into. Amy would have driven any man with less character up the wall long ago. She gave me a hard enough time, God knows, when I married her mother. And since too."

Lambert stood up and went over to the bar to replenish his glass. "Another Coke?" he asked over his shoulder.

"No thanks, plenty left."

"Well, I certainly need a quick refill. Had a hard day. They're pulling me every which way on this revitalization thing."

He made himself another stiff drink and returned to his chair. "I take it you're not getting anywhere with that prowler," he said.

"He doesn't seem too promising, sir."

"And that yardman we heard about? I forget his name—"

"Corley. He's not too promising either."

"But it has to be someone like that. Not Paul."

"I hope he appreciates what a loyal supporter he has in you, sir."

"Oh, we've always got on well." Lambert picked up his glass, drank and added, "He'll certainly be easier to deal with where this house is concerned. I'm sure you know, checking things out, that my late wife," a shadow touched his face, "left me life use of it and that it then went to my stepdaughter. Now, of course, to Paul. Amy created problems over it every chance she had." He shook his head.

"Poor girl, she never forgave me for marrying her mother. But that's water over the dam now . . ."

Morris, still going through the motions, said, "Getting back to Mrs. Gardner's death, sir—have you remembered anything at all that you could add to your original statement on it?"

"I'm afraid not," Lambert replied. "Lord knows I've thought about it enough too. But as I said in my statement, I hadn't seen Amy for almost a week before her death or even talked to her on the phone. It came from out of the blue, Paul's phone call that night soon after I got home from a meeting at the Lafayette Inn. You know, the Downtown—" He broke off with a smile. "But of course you know. I'm sure that as well as checking on Paul, you've also investigated my whereabouts that night."

"Matter of routine, sir."

"Yes. And a matter of luck for me—I wish Paul could share it—that I was at that meeting. Any other night I might easily have been right here at home with no one to vouch for me."

"Even if you were, the burden of proof would still be on us, sir, that you left your house, went to Mrs. Gardner's and killed her."

"Great comfort, Anglo-Saxon law," Lambert said.

Morris turned the subject to Luke Welford.

"Real likable guy," Lambert responded. "Came here a lot years ago. Not in Paul's league, though. More . . . well, my father had an expression you don't hear much nowadays. He'd say so-and-so was okay but not much bottom to him."

"Substance, character?" Morris conjectured.

"Something like that—not quite that strong, maybe. At least not where Luke's concerned. He's a very able bright young man. A little happy-go-lucky, not as considerate of other people as he could be. Crazy about his aunt Stella. He was the one person, as I recall it, that Amy ever accepted sharing her mother with. But then she was crazy about Luke herself."

"How did he feel toward her?"

"Well . . ." Lambert shrugged. "Put up with her in her teens, found her less of a nuisance, I'd say, as they both got older. But he's dropped off coming here since my wife," again the shadow, "died. In fact, we hardly saw him in recent years until Amy's death. He's been around more lately. Not surprising that he stayed away, feeling as he did about his aunt Stella . . ."

Lambert drained his glass and set it aside. Then he said, "Everyone who knew her fell in love with her. Including me. Above all, me." A deep flush came to his face. His voice broke. "I never really—got over losing her."

Morris murmured sympathy, a little embarrassed—was it Lambert's two quick drinks working on him?—by this sudden display of emotion.

He had no more questions to ask and left a few minutes later.

Lambert, he felt, could be crossed off. That left Gardner and Luke Welford—or did it? For all he knew, it could be someone not even on their list.

That was a disheartening thought. He shook it off. See what tomorrow, when he was to check on Welford in Alexandria, would bring.

CHAPTER NINETEEN

The temperature had reached the high seventies that Thursday, more like summer than April, but there was a pleasant breeze blowing off Occaquan Creek when Rachel and her father-in-law moved out onto the porch after Griffin's excellent dinner.

Rachel was content to sit in silence looking out at the distant creek, a curve of silver in the fading light. They hadn't talked about her husband at dinner except for Arthur Carey's brief reference to a phone conversation with him Sunday. She hadn't heard from Neil herself in nearly three weeks. The cautious hope was growing in her that there would be no more distressing calls from him that either blamed her for their impending divorce or sought a reconciliation.

But Neil seemed far away during this tranquil interval; as far away as Amy Gardner's murder.

Rachel had said little about Paul Gardner's visit to her last night and made no mention of going to his house tomorrow. Her father-in-law would only express disapproval that she didn't want to hear. She had let him have his say yesterday about her involvement in the case.

As if she could have helped it.

But she could certainly help seeing Paul Gardner again. Except that she looked forward to it, felt drawn to him in a way.

Was he drawn to her a little too?

It wasn't right, it was much too soon to entertain such thoughts.

But at least she now felt certain, after his soul-searching last night, the sense of guilt he displayed over the deterioration of his marriage, that he hadn't brought it to an end himself by killing his wife. That had been no act last night, put on for her benefit.

Two late-homing mockingbirds distracted Rachel's attention just then, scolding each other raucously as they lit in a clump of shrubbery out in front.

She laughed. "Listen to that."

Arthur Carey eyed the birds resignedly. "They're checking to see how the berries on the mahonia bushes are coming along. Nothing they like better. The minute the berries ripen they'll strip them clean."

The birds flew off to bed and silence reigned again. In the deepening twilight Rachel felt at peace with herself.

Morris's trip to Alexandria Friday morning was to no purpose. Accompanied by a detective from the Alexandria force, he made the rounds in Luke's apartment building, questioning his neighbors, talking to the manager and maintenance men and ending up where he had started. No one had phoned Luke the night of the murder or called on him; no one had seen him leave the building or return to it.

He made a list of those who weren't home. They would have to be checked later but as things stood, he reported back to Betz, there was no evidence either way on Welford's statement that he had been home all that evening.

"We're getting nowhere fast," Betz commented sourly.

"Right, sir," said Morris.

Betz scowled at him and uttered more sour words.

Morris felt injured. Hell, the way the captain acted, anyone would think it was all his fault. What was he supposed to do, pull rabbits out of a hat?

When Rachel arrived at Paul Gardner's that afternoon he barely had time to greet her before he had to go answer the phone.

He had taken her into the living room. It ran the depth of the house with windows front and side and a French door opening onto a brick-paved patio in back.

Rachel moved around it, absorbing the layout and furnishings, the fireplace with the raised hearth and huge old brass andirons, the delicately faded oriental rugs, furniture that was a mixture of old and new, all blending comfortably together.

It was a lovely restful room, Rachel thought, good taste prevailing down to the last detail. Whatever problems the dead girl had were not reflected in her home.

As this thought crossed her mind, Paul Gardner spoke from the doorway. "Let me fix you a drink, Rachel. Scotch, isn't it?"

"Yes." She turned to face him. "I like this room."

"I do too. Always have. Amy's mother helped with it. With the whole house, for that matter. It was her last project, just finished when she died and nothing changed since . . . I'll get our drinks."

Rachel looked around again seeing the room in a different light now that she had been told it wasn't a reflection of Amy's personality but of Mrs. Lambert's. Her taste and influence still prevailed from the grave.

Poor Amy, Rachel thought. She had lived in her mother's shadow until her life ended.

The house was quiet. All she could hear was the grandfather clock ticking in the hall and remoter sounds of drinks being made in the kitchen.

She went out onto the patio and sat down. A fat brown and white cat stretched out nearby glared at her and stalked away. It must be Brindle.

Somewhere not too far away a power mower was cutting grass. Here the lawn spreading out from foundation plantings to the close-growing shrubbery bordering it on both sides and in the rear looked freshly mowed. The yardman who was in trouble with Betz was still employed, it seemed, by Paul Gardner.

"Your yard looks so well kept," she said when he came out with their drinks.

"Corley was here yesterday. I've been giving him a lot of thought." He paused. "It's quite possible, I feel, that Amy did give him her engagement ring in a fit of temper at me."

"Have you told the police that?" Rachel inquired.

He shook his head. "I haven't talked with them about it since they first picked Corley up and asked me if I thought Amy might have given him the ring. It jarred me so that I said no at the time but now I'm not so sure."

"Oh. Are you going to tell them that?"

"When I get to it. Right now," an edge came into his voice, "I just want to stay as far away from them as I can."

The cat appearing around the corner of the house offered a safer topic. "Isn't that Brindle?" Rachel asked.

"Yes." Paul Gardner whistled and the cat sauntered over at its own pace to have its head scratched.

They finished their drinks. When he suggested a refill, Rachel looked at her watch and said, "No, thank you, I'm afraid I haven't the time. I'm on Hot Line tonight and I have to get home and fix dinner first."

"Well then, I'd better show you the dresses now." He got to his feet.

They went inside and down the hall turning into a short passageway that led into the bedroom wing of the house.

There were three bedrooms. Two stood open, the third was closed. He opened the third door and said, "This used to be our room. I've moved into another one."

It was a large corner room, windows shut, curtains drawn, a bathroom off it. A faint scent of perfume lingered in the air, perhaps from toiletries on the dressing table.

Paul Gardner turned on a light and opened one of two closet doors, pressing the light switch just outside the door.

"Party dresses are in back to your left," he said and retreated to the doorway as if reluctant to remain in the room.

There was no lack of clothes, Rachel saw, hanging from

the pole that stretched the full width of the closet; or of shoes helter-skelter in the shoe rack on the floor.

She moved hangers to reach the evening dresses. They were not in plastic bags or even hung carefully, just pushed back out of the way; one of them, a fragile chiffon, half off its hanger. As if, Rachel thought, Amy had lost all interest in the kind of parties they were intended for and would never wear any of them again.

She felt awkward looking through the dresses, the scent of the dead girl's perfume around her, her presence almost tangible in the closed-up room.

Had she called Rachel that last time from the phone on the bedside stand?

How would she regard Rachel now—as an intruder, grave robber, picking over her clothes?

That was a morbid thought. After all, Rachel was here at Paul Gardner's invitation—

She glanced at him as she carried an armload of dresses over to the bed. He still stood in the doorway watching her, his face without expression.

She spread out the dresses, a rainbow of colors from the pale yellow chiffon to a rich-looking red silk, each of them simple in design but of excellent quality and workmanship.

"They're all lovely," she said.

He gave them a brief glance. "I hope they're still in style. They go back to before we were married and we haven't gone many places for Amy to wear them since."

He said nothing more while Rachel looked over the dresses, all size eight and all expensive beyond the dreams of the girl who was to have one of them.

The silence became oppressive. Rachel heard herself say, "The things you think of sometimes. I've been wondering if Amy called me that last time from the phone in here."

"It would depend on where she was when she made the call," Paul Gardner replied. "There are three phones in the house."

"I know. Just a pointless thought." She picked up a deep blue dress of some soft silky material and held it in front of her while she looked in a mirror.

"This one," she said. "It's young-looking and it's beautiful." She laid it aside and hung the rest back in the closet.

"Shouldn't the girl have things to go with it?" he asked. "Like shoes and a bag?"

"We don't know her shoe size."

"Oh, that's right. But there are a lot of evening bags in that chest over there." Without moving from the doorway—he had a real thing about this room, Rachel thought—he gestured toward an old pine chest against the far wall. "They're in the bottom drawer, I think."

Another intrusion on Amy's possessions. But still, the girl would love having an evening bag to go with the dress. Rachel went over to the chest, opened the bottom drawer and found a lavish array to choose from.

A small silver brocaded bag seemed just right. There should be silver slippers, too, but the girl would have to manage those herself.

Rachel opened the bag. There was a zipper compartment, a fluff of lint at the bottom, that was all.

"This will be fine," she said, slipping the mesh chain over her arm and picking up the dress. "It's so nice of you, Paul," she added giving him a warm smile. "The girl will be thrilled to death."

"Let's hope she has a good time wearing the dress." He still blocked the doorway as Rachel approached it. His face tightened suddenly.

She hesitated. For a heart-stopping moment she didn't know whether he was going to kiss her or grab her by the throat.

He did neither. He stood aside at the last moment and let her precede him along the passageway into the hall. A small prickle between her shoulder blades bore witness to Rachel's own tightened nerves.

But everything returned to normal as he opened the front door for her. Looking out into the late afternoon sunshine it seemed to Rachel that the incident just past was a product of her imagination, conjured up by the haunted atmosphere in the dead girl's room.

She put it firmly out of her mind and said, "My pocket-book—did I leave it in the car? Yes, I did."

"It's nice you have so much faith in my neighbors' honesty," he remarked walking her out to her car.

"Justified—see?" She pointed to her pocketbook on the seat.

Neither of them gave more than a fleeting glance at a tall blond boy walking past just then. They had no way of knowing that it was Amy's prowler, Peter Jackson. He looked at them out of the corner of his eye and at Brindle stretched out near the front steps.

Rachel thanked Paul Gardner again as she got into her car and started it.

"Glad to help out," he said. "You'll have to tell me sometime if the girl liked the dress."

The implication was there that they would see each other again.

Well, that was what she wanted.

She thought about it, driving slowly along Britton Road while home-going cars, red, green, white, blue, moved past her in a steady procession. Next time, though, there mustn't be any tense moments.

She found a box the dress would fit in when she got home. She started to lay the brocaded bag on top of it, remembered the fluff of lint inside and opened it. Paper in the zipper compartment rustled as she removed the lint. She slid back the zipper and took it out.

It was an oblong sheet of good quality paper folded in half. Centered at the top was the letterhead of a Philadelphia jeweler with a Chestnut Street address, a good

address, Rachel recalled from her college days in Philadelphia.

Dated November 11, 1971, it was addressed to Mr. Brian
Grady, P. O. Box 975, Alexandria, Virginia, 22313. It read:

Dear Mr. Grady:

In regard to the antique pendant you left with us recently, made up of one star ruby (approximate weight
5.25 carats) surrounded by a cluster of cushion cut diamonds (total weight of same, approximately 6.75 carats)
set in platinum, our appraiser considers that a fair and
reasonable offer for the pendant would be ten thousand
dollars. If this is satisfactory to you, we can complete the
transaction when you are next in Philadelphia—which you
mentioned, I believe, will be the week of November 22. If
the offer does not suit you, we will then return the pendant to you.

Very truly yours,
James B. Wilson

Rachel's first reaction was puzzlement that Amy Gardner
should have carried the letter around in her evening bag.
Not her letter either, but addressed to a Mr. Brian Grady,
whoever he was. How had she got hold of it?

Rachel read it again, her puzzlement increasing as she
looked at the date. In November 1971 Amy's mother was
dead for over a year but from what Paul Gardner had said,
they didn't go to many parties where Amy would have been
dressed up enough to carry the brocaded bag.

It seemed more likely that she had used it as a safe place
to keep the letter where it wouldn't get mixed up with any
other papers.

In other words, it was important to her.

But why? The letter wasn't her property any more than
the pendant was. Both belonged to the unknown Mr. Grady
whom Rachel had never heard mentioned in connection
with the dead girl.

Jewelry, though, was connected with her mother's death . . .

Rachel tried to remember what Amy had told her about it. But it had come up during one of their earlier conversations, perhaps two months ago and she could no longer recall it in detail. All that remained clear was that Mrs. Lambert had shown her daughter various pieces of jewelry stolen later that night by the prowler who killed her.

Could the antique pendant have been one of them?

But if that were the case, would Mr. Grady have been offering it for sale to a reputable jeweler in Philadelphia? There were shadier, less risky ways to dispose of stolen jewelry, weren't there?

It seemed more logical to assume that Mr. Grady hadn't sold the pendant to the jeweler and had later got a better price for it from Amy Gardner who could certainly afford to buy it if it struck her fancy. Mr. Grady might well have turned the letter, with its description of the pendant, over to her at the time of the sale. Amy might then, perhaps on a temporary basis, have put it in the brocaded bag for safekeeping apart from other papers.

Papers . . . Why did that suddenly ring a bell?

Rachel had no idea. It didn't matter anyway. She'd had enough of speculation for the time being. She would just call Paul Gardner and tell him what she had found. He might clear it all up in a minute. In any case, she would have to return the letter to him.

She looked up his number and dialed it. The line was busy. She waited for an interval and dialed again. This time it was free but the man who answered wasn't Paul Gardner. She asked to speak to him.

"He just left," the man said. "Wait a minute, though, and I'll see if I can catch him."

Rachel waited.

The man came back. "Sorry, his car was turning down the street when I got outside. This is Frank Lambert speaking, by the way. I was on the way out myself when you called."

"Oh. This is Rachel Carey, Mr. Lambert. We met—"

"I remember. Paul was telling me you were here a little while ago to get a dress for some girl. I had to make a phone call and he left ahead of me. Can I take a message for him?"

"Well, just that I called and will get in touch another time. It's not urgent. It's just to tell him I found a letter he might want back in an evening bag of Mrs. Gardner's."

"I see. I won't try to put that down, though. I'll just leave a note that you called."

"That will do fine. Thank you, Mr. Lambert." Rachel said good-by and hung up.

Before she started dinner she put the letter away in a desk drawer.

CHAPTER TWENTY

Rachel made it a point to arrive at the Hot Line office a few minutes early that night. She parked her car in back, took out the dress box and crossed the street with it to Lafayette Inn.

She was on friendly terms with the desk clerk who said he would keep the box to be called for.

"What name?" he asked.

"I don't know her name and she doesn't know mine. But there'll only be one girl, I'm sure, coming in to get it."

"Well, I'd better stick a note on it in case she shows up when I'm not here," he said. "I've got a pad around somewhere mixed up with all these papers." He started rummaging around.

Papers . . . That word again jogging her memory. It followed her across the street into the Hot Line office.

She took her first call of the evening. Right after it, sitting back in the chair, Rachel suddenly remembered why the word had meaning for her. The last time Amy Gardner had called her with death only an hour or two away she had said something about old family papers; that she was going to finish looking through them before she went outside to watch for the prowler.

Old family papers. But the letter couldn't have been among them. It was too recent for that.

The phone rang. Rachel referred the caller, seeking information on adoption proceedings, to the appropriate agency and returned to her musings.

Whatever the papers were, they must have come under

police scrutiny after Amy's murder, been inspected and set aside as having no bearing on the case.

The search hadn't been thorough enough, however, for the letter to be found. When the police had looked in the brocaded bag—if they ever had—they had probably assumed it was empty as Rachel had herself the first time she opened it.

But the family papers were a different matter. They must have been right at hand in a desk or box or something for Amy to have been examining them not long before her death. That was why there could be no doubt that the police had seen them.

Nevertheless, having told Captain Betz that she would let him know if she remembered what Amy Gardner had said she was doing that night, Rachel called him on the unlisted phone.

He was off duty, the desk man said. She could reach him after eight in the morning or was there anyone else who could help her?

"I'll call in the morning," Rachel said.

The office phone rang. It was the girl who had called the other night about the dress.

She poured out her thanks ecstatically when she learned that Rachel had found a dress and an evening bag for her. She would get her father to drive her to Lafayette Inn right away to pick it up, she said.

The girl, still bubbling, got off the phone at last.

The next call came from an adolescent boy, voice quavering with laughter as he asked, "Do you know where Lake Amston is?"

"Oh yes," said Rachel and then, stealing his line, "But why don't you go jump in it instead of me? You don't seem to have much else to keep you busy."

"Hey—how'd you know—?"

"Because once upon a time I was your age too," she replied and hung up.

She was smiling to herself as she made out a daily sheet on the call. It was a rare week that she didn't get a joke call —or, on the ugly side—an obscene one.

Other aides, comparing notes with her, had the same experience.

The phone rang frequently for the next hour. When a lull came around nine-thirty her thoughts turned to her date tomorrow night with Luke Welford, the possibility of an awkward moment or two when he arrived. They hadn't seen each other since he had told her about his long-ago affair with Amy Gardner. He might, of course, just take it in his stride.

No matter how he acted, she liked him the less for the telling of what was, everything considered, a sordid little business better kept to himself.

Had Paul Gardner ever found out about it? She hoped not. She couldn't imagine him mixed up in anything like that himself.

The phone rang. She picked it up. "Hot Line, Martha speaking. Can I help you?"

In the upstairs hall, seated on a chair that stood against the wall, Lambert waited in the shadows invisible from below in the dim light that filtered up the stairs. He waited for time to pass, for the traffic outside to dwindle to a trickle as the hour grew later, for pedestrians abroad to go home to bed. He waited for the Hot Line phone to quiet down— surely it stopped ringing long before midnight brought someone else to take Rachel Carey's place?

He could hear it every now and then, a faint sound in the solidly built old house.

He had come in the front door half an hour ago, foot- steps noiseless in sneakers as he climbed the stairs and moved the hall chair close to the bathroom, his line of re- treat in case one of the tenants appeared.

None did. He hadn't thought they would. All the offices

except Hot Line were in darkness Tuesday night, too, when he had scouted the building.

It had been no more than a small nagging worry that had brought him here then, stemming from the fact that he had parked his car out in back the night of that ill-starred dinner meeting at Lafayette Inn. He had often left it there before, knowing how limited the parking was at the inn and, as city planner, knowing the location of almost every private parking lot in Monmouth—just as he had known, since it first opened, that this was where the Hot Line office was located.

What he hadn't known when he parked there that night was that within the next few hours he would have to kill Amy.

And then, at quarter of nine or so, the dinner over, the guest speaker launched on his speech, a waiter had approached to tell him he was wanted on the phone.

As always when he could manage it, he had picked a corner table where he could slip out through the cloakroom into the hall and around to the bar if the speaker was too long-winded. He was lucky in that when the call came and luckier still that the only others at his table were two city planners from out of town.

He excused himself to them and left unnoticed through the cloakroom to take the call at the desk in the lobby. It was Amy.

Waiting there in the upstairs hall, nerves on edge, Lambert's thoughts went back to what followed.

"Frank?" Amy said when he picked up.

"Yes."

"This is Amy." Her voice was sharp, high-pitched. "I've been going through some old papers I brought home from Mother's the other day and I just came across a letter that was mixed in with them from a jeweler in Philadelphia. It's addressed to a Mr. Grady. Did you ever hear of him?"

"No," he said but God, how his heart sank. That letter,

mislaid two years ago, accidentally destroyed he had hoped
—that letter.

Ruby, of course. Ruby, who threw out nothing, must have
picked it up somewhere in the house and put it among
other papers in Stella's desk.

"Frank, it describes Great-Grandma Lundy's ruby and
diamond pendant—no question about it—and the jeweler
is offering to buy it for ten thousand dollars. It was one of
the pieces Mother had out the night she was killed—don't
you remember that? The prowler stole it with the rest. How
could it have turned up in Philadelphia and how did the
letter about it get in among Mother's papers?"

His mind raced. This was the greatest crisis he had ever
faced and had to be resolved immediately.

"I have no idea," he said. "But look, I'll leave now and
be right out. Don't call anyone else, don't do anything until
I get there and see the letter for myself. Then we'll figure
out what to do."

"All right," Amy said, "as long as you come right away."

"I will. This minute."

He hung up. The desk clerk was in conversation with
someone at the other end of the desk. Lambert didn't call
attention to himself by saying thank you. He hurried down
the hall, out the side door and across the street to get his
car.

No one saw him. The curtains were drawn at the front
windows of the Hot Line office, the rest of the building was
in darkness as he ran along the driveway beside it. But the
kitchen window in back overlooking the parking lot was
uncurtained and the shade was only drawn down to the
middle sash. It began to worry him as soon as he met Rachel
Carey and learned of her involvement with Amy. Not because at some point she might have seen his car parked out
there; that was all right. What worried him was that she
might have looked out again later on and noticed that it
was gone. A Corvette was a noticeable car.

He had even thought of selling it after he met her but that seemed excessive. For one thing, she didn't know what kind of a car he drove and with their paths not likely to cross never would; for another thing, she might not have seen his car at all that night.

For him to sell it suddenly when he'd bought it just a few months ago and talked about how much he liked it would have involved him in elaborate explanations.

So he had let it go. . . .

He drove fast to Amy's. He knew, as he had known from the moment she mentioned the letter, that he had to kill her as soon as he got it in his hands. Grady, the name he had used negotiating the sale of the pendant, was paper-thin cover once Amy started pursuing the matter as she surely would.

The only real anonymity he'd ever had in the affair was through paying cash for the post office box he rented in Alexandria, the nearest city of any size.

If only he had thrown the goddamn pendant away with the rest of the jewelry he had taken that other time to make it look as if a chance prowler had killed Stella.

Stella . . . He had loved her as he had loved no other woman before or since. Beautiful, unpredictable, enchanting Stella—how could he have given her up to someone else? And yet that was what she had expected, that she could discard him, the husband who adored her, as easily as a dress she no longer wanted to wear.

He had never known, never tried to find out who his replacement was to be. That he existed, that Stella wanted a divorce to marry him was enough to know, coming home a little early from his meeting that night, going upstairs, finding Stella's unfinished letter to her unknown lover on her desk, she in the bathroom, running water covering up the sounds of his arrival.

When she opened the bathroom door he was standing there, numb with shock, the letter in his hand.

"Well," she said in a wry tone, "I didn't want you to find out this way, but there's really no easy way, is there, to tell you our marriage is over?"

He went wild then begging her to reconsider. He shouted, pleaded, all but groveled in his insistence that she tell him what was the matter, what he needed to change about himself to keep their marriage going.

It was no use. There was nothing he could do, she said. She had fallen in love with someone else, she was tired of him, she just wanted a divorce.

After she said that he lost all control of himself, picked up a heavy copper figurine on her desk, hit her with it, pursued her out into the hall as she ran screaming from him. He hit her again and again in blind fury until her screams stopped . . .

He wanted to die at first himself when he realized he had killed her.

The pendant was among the pieces of jewelry spread out on Stella's dressing table, the most valuable of them all. He had swept it up with the rest, put them in a paper bag and run outside to thrust them deep into a nearby culvert with a rock weighting them down. Then he had called the police.

Over a week passed before he felt safe in retrieving them and driving out into the country along the Potomac to drop them in one by one. All except the pendant. Practical considerations took over as he looked and looked at it, knowing it was valued at twenty thousand on the insurance list. If he kept it in his safe deposit box for a year or two he could sell it for at least half its appraised value somewhere well away from Monmouth. Stella owed it to him after what she had done. Added to what she had left him in her will, it would help him with the house which was going to be expensive to maintain.

So he had kept the pendant and sold it a year later in Philadelphia.

That was the end of it, he had thought, but now there

was Amy, a repeat of that other time, just as ugly and with just as many risks involved.

She was waiting at the back door when he got out of his car.

"Well, let's see the letter," he said as soon as they were inside.

"No hurry," she replied.

She was in one of her difficult moods, he saw.

"What d'you mean, no hurry?" He tried to sound matter-of-fact, restraining wild impatience. "You got me out here to see it."

"Did I?" She sauntered over to a counter and leaned against it. "It's in the bag, Frank, and won't go away." She laughed on a willful note. "I got over the first shock of the letter after I called you and then I began thinking about how it could have got mixed in with Mother's papers. Have you been thinking about it, too, on the way here?"

"Yes, but I haven't figured it out yet."

She wasn't laughing now. "You and Ruby and I were the only people who had access to Mother's desk. I know I didn't put the letter there. Did you, Frank? Did Ruby? It has to be one of us—or did the mysterious Mr. Grady come in through the window?"

His mouth was so dry that he had to swallow before he managed to say, "I don't know what the answer is."

"Someone does. Was Mr. Grady the prowler who killed Mother?"

He swallowed again. "If you'll just show me the letter—"

"I've told you what's in it. A description of the pendant, an offer to pay ten thousand for it." Amy shook back her long dark hair staring at him fixedly. "You must have some thoughts on it, Frank."

"A phony letter, some sort of hoax?"

"Oh no," she said incisively. "There is such a jeweler at the address given. I called Philadelphia information on it just before you came. I tried their phone number but of course there was no one there at this time of night."

She walked across the room and back, a slender girl, feather light. Leaning against the counter again she said, "I'll tell you how I've got that letter worked out, Frank. I think the prowler panicked that night when he realized he had killed Mother and dropped the pendant while he was making his getaway. I think you found it when you got home either before you called the police or before they arrived and regardless of how upset you were hid it away somewhere."

Amy paused to take a cigarette out of a pack on the counter and light it before she added reflectively, "Maybe you weren't actually thinking about its cash value at the moment. Maybe it was just to keep me from having it—because we were always jealous of each other where Mother was concerned, weren't we?"

Relief flooded through him that Amy was only accusing him of theft. What if he admitted it, offered to make restitution if, for her mother's sake, she would keep it quiet, keep the police out of it?

Above all, that. The police wouldn't be ready to settle for theft. They would reopen their investigation of Stella's death and even though they could find no proof that he had killed her, there would be all kinds of unpleasant publicity, a scandal that would cost him his job and hang over him the rest of his life.

Would Amy let him give her back the money and keep it quiet? Christ, would she?

He was never to know the answer to that question. Her gaze—she had hardly taken her eyes off him since his arrival—narrowed.

"You look—almost pleased, Frank," she said in a choked voice. "Pleased to be called a thief? Why? I thought—I expected you to hit the ceiling."

"I'm too stunned by what you said."

"No, that's not it!" She shook her head violently. "That's not it at all. You don't look stunned, you don't look anything right now. But for a minute there you did look pleased—or rather—" She broke off groping for the word she wanted.

Suddenly it came to her. "Relieved, that's it! That's how you looked. But why? Oh, my God—my God—" Her face went rigid with horror. "Because the truth is so much worse, that's why! Because you killed my mother yourself!"

"Amy—" He took a step toward her.

"Stay away from me," she cried, and ran to the back door.

He caught up with her before she reached it, grabbed the doorstop and with one blow . . .

She didn't have the letter on her. Fighting squeamishness —thank God there was little blood, none on him—he forced himself to search her for it. Frantic over the passage of time, his need to get back to Lafayette Inn and establish an alibi, he made a hasty search of the obvious places, desk and drawers and cupboards, snatching up in the bedroom a handful of jewelry—Christ, how history repeated itself— and then had to leave to get back to the meeting. This time he was able to park right outside and slip back into the din- ing room by the side door. While he was away killing Amy the speaker had gone right on talking and was just at that point bringing his speech to a close.

He was one of the first to congratulate the speaker and then went around greeting people before he settled in the bar with friends.

He had his alibi but he didn't know how much good it would do him if the letter turned up.

He had made frequent visits to Paul ever since trying to find it. This afternoon he had dropped in on him, knowing he was going out to dinner somewhere before his classes, and had used the phone as an excuse to stay on after he left, planning to make the most thorough search of all.

Then had come the bombshell of Rachel Carey's call.

He couldn't let her give the letter to Paul. That was why

he was here. But God, he thought, it seemed as if one death just led to another.

All Stella's fault. If she had been as faithful to him as he was to her, none of this would have happened.

It had to stop. It would stop tonight. This would be the end of it. With the gun that had belonged to Stella's first husband he would make sure that it was.

Before his luck ran out.

It couldn't last forever.

CHAPTER TWENTY-ONE

At quarter of eleven, the phone quiet, Rachel went out into the kitchen to make herself a cup of coffee.

Turning on the faucet, she was brought up short by a series of crashes followed by the cry of "Help!"

Without stopping to think, she did the natural instinctive thing, rushed to the door and opened it.

Lambert stood just outside.

In one hand he held a gun pointed at her. The other rested on the back of the chair he had thrown down the stairs.

"I'll have to ask you to carry this back up for me, Mrs. Carey," he said. "It's not heavy, though, just a straight wooden chair."

"But—" She stared at him unbelievingly.

"The chair, Mrs. Carey." He tested it. "Back leg seems wobbly but I doubt it gets much use anyway."

Only the gun was real. Rachel picked up the chair and started slowly up the stairs, Lambert close behind her. When she hesitated on the way debating her chances if she turned suddenly and shoved the chair in his face, he seemed to read her mind, prodding her with the gun, saying abruptly, "No tricks, Mrs. Carey. This gun is loaded."

And there was no one to hear if he shot her, Rachel thought numbly. She carried the chair the rest of the way up, putting it where he had found it in the upstairs hall.

A scream wouldn't be heard either. She preceded him downstairs and into the Hot Line office.

If the phone would only ring—but it stood mute on the desk.

"Now if you'll just get your pocketbook, Mrs. Carey—that's yours, isn't it, over there on the chair?"

"Yes."

He took it from her nerveless hand, searched it thoroughly without finding the letter and removed her keys.

"What did you do with Amy's letter?" he asked.

So that was it. Of course. Amy's letter.

She hesitated. Say she had already mailed it to Paul Gardner? He wouldn't believe her.

"It's home," she said.

"All right, we'll go get it . . . This yours?" He picked up her suede jacket thrown over the back of the chair.

Rachel stood rooted by the desk. "I can't leave now, Mr. Lambert. Not until the woman who takes over at midnight arrives. Hot Line has to be covered twenty-four hours a day."

But it was a meaningless statement, Rachel knew, even as she made it. What did he care about Hot Line?

"Too bad," he said. "What's your relief's name?"

"Mrs. Tyler." A flicker of hope sprang up. If he would let her call Mrs. Tyler to offer some excuse she might be able to—

But again he seemed to read her mind. "Leave a note," he said. "Tell her there was an emergency, someone came to get you and you had to leave a few minutes early."

Rachel wrote the note. He read it to make sure there was nothing added to signal her plight.

"Okay, let's go," he said.

She picked up her pocketbook, draped her jacket over her shoulders and sent a last desperate glance around the room. If there were just some way to let Mrs. Tyler know—

But what was she thinking of? Of course Mrs. Tyler would know something was wrong the moment she arrived and found the door locked. She would know that if Rachel had to leave early she would call Mrs. Holt or her assistant and that one of them would have to be there to let Mrs. Tyler in.

Lambert didn't know that. He would assume that Hot Line aides had their own keys to the office. It wouldn't occur to him that they needed none with someone always there to admit them.

Rachel was momentarily heartened by the thought that Mrs. Tyler would call Mrs. Holt immediately and that she, in turn, would lose no time calling the police.

But as Lambert closed the office door behind them and took a firm grip on Rachel's arm her ray of hope died. What could the police do, after all? It would be another hour before they even heard about what had happened. They would check her apartment, yes, but it didn't seem likely that Lambert would just leave her there to greet them when they appeared. And where else could they look for her in the middle of the night?

Lambert opened the front door and glanced out. No one in sight, only one car approaching. He waited until it passed and then rushed Rachel down the front steps and around in back to the parking lot.

His car was parked at the far end of the lot. Rachel stopped short as they came close to it, a blue Corvette.

"That's your car?" The question burst from her in sudden realization. "The one that was here part of the time the night—" She broke off, caution taking over too late.

"So you did see it that night, Mrs. Carey," Lambert remarked.

She tried to cover up her mistake. "I meant when I arrived. I didn't notice how long it was—" She broke off again. She was only making matters worse.

He opened the door on the driver's side and took out his keys. "You drive," he said. "You might try to jump out if I do. Automatic transmission, no problem even if you're not used to this kind of car."

Rachel got in behind the wheel, a doomed feeling settling over her. She had sealed her fate with all that she had blurted out about his car, condemned herself out of her own mouth—

No, she thought, as he got in on the passenger side and handed her the keys. She had been doomed from the start, from the moment she opened the door of the Hot Line office and found him outside. He would not have been there at all if he hadn't meant to kill her.

It was because of the letter. He had killed Amy Gardner over it and now that she knew about it he meant to kill her too.

Her recognition of his car was a happenstance thing, no more than a footnote to the letter.

If only she hadn't mentioned it to him this afternoon or if she hadn't been so easily tricked into opening the door tonight . . .

If. What was the use of that? It wouldn't help her to escape from this horrible predicament she had blundered into.

There was no escape from it. Franklin Lambert, settling himself beside her, the gun held loosely in his right hand, intended to kill her. The only thing that had kept him from it right there in the Hot Line office was that he wanted to get hold of the letter first.

As she started the motor, Rachel began to shake all over terrified by the prospect of her own imminent death. Her teeth chattered. Her foot slipped off the gas pedal.

"I can't drive this car," she protested. "I just can't. How can you expect it, the state I'm in? Look at my hands shake." She held them out for him to see.

"Cut out the hysterics," Lambert said sharply. "You have nothing to fear as long as you do as you're told. This gun is just to keep you in line. I have no intention of using it unless you force me to. So relax now and let's get going to your apartment."

Rachel's will to live made her want to believe him. After a moment she drew in a deep breath and put the car in gear.

The street was deserted when she drove out onto it. The traffic light ahead turned red as she approached it. Now all she needed was a police car to come along and she would run through it.

None came. There were no other cars at all in sight. She slowed to a stop.

Lambert was silent. What were his thoughts?

The light turned green. Rachel drove on taking the familiar turns toward home. There was little traffic at that hour but hope stirred again as she drew near her apartment house and saw a man getting out of his car in the parking lot beside it.

Lambert saw him too. "Drive past and turn back at the next corner," he said. "That will give him time to get inside."

The man was gone when she drove into the parking lot. No one else appeared as they got out of the car, Lambert gripping her arm again on the way into the foyer and upstairs to her apartment. He gave Rachel her keys to unlock the door and motioned her in ahead of him, telling her to turn on the lights.

When they were in the living room he had her draw the curtains and then said, "Now get the letter, Mrs. Carey."

There was nothing to be gained by stalling. She went over to the desk and got the letter out of the drawer.

Lambert glanced at it, took out his cigarette lighter and burned it in an ash tray.

"Where's the kitchen?" he asked.

"Down the hall."

He handed her the ash tray. "You go first."

He stood over her while she washed and dried it, rinsing charred bits of paper down the drain.

"Now put it back where it was, Mrs. Carey," he said.

A fresh wave of terror assailed Rachel as they returned to the living room. The letter, her one safeguard, had been disposed of. Now he was free to kill her as he had intended all along.

Her knees gave way. She collapsed into the nearest chair.

He watched her closely. "This won't do, Mrs. Carey," he said. "We've got to get moving."

"No," she said. "You're going to kill me anyway so why should I make it easier for you by letting you take me to some quiet spot where no one will hear the gun?"

"Don't be a fool," he retorted. "I've got enough to worry about without killing you. All I want from you now is co-operation so that I can get a good head start."

She huddled deeper in the chair. "Head start for what?"

"On the police, of course. You don't think I'm just going to walk out of here and have you calling them before I'm a block away, do you?" He shook his head firmly. "No indeed. What I have in mind is to take you out onto some country road miles from anywhere and put you out of the car. I expect to be at least a hundred miles away before you reach a place where you can spread the alarm."

Lambert's curt impatient tone carried conviction. He was a good actor.

In any case, Rachel, clinging desperately to life, wanted to believe him.

"Come on now," he added sharply. "I haven't got all night."

She got shakily to her feet, all too aware of the gun in his hand. He hadn't put it down once since they had entered her apartment; even while he was burning the letter he had kept it in his right hand. Other things, like unlocking the door and washing the ash tray, had been assigned to her. He was taking no chances at all with her.

"Don't forget your pocketbook," he reminded her as she started toward the door. "You'll need money to get home from where I'll be taking you."

The reminder cheered her as Lambert intended it should. It really seemed that he was going to let her go, she thought.

He was right behind her when she opened the door, halting her while he looked out and listened. There was no one in the hall. The only sound came from a television set behind one of the closed doors.

It wasn't right that he should have all this good luck, Rachel thought resentfully as he rushed her down the stairs and out to his car. Someone should show up going in or out of the building.

But no one did.

Lambert opened the car door and handed her his keys. "You're still driving," he said.

Rachel started the motor. "Head south out of town," he said, "and take the turnoff to Route 1. I want to look over country roads out that way."

To be put out of a car on a country road in the middle of the night would have been a frightening prospect, Rachel thought, under any other circumstances. But tonight just to see the last of Lambert and his gun, the taillights of his car vanishing in the distance, leaving her behind on a dark and lonely country road, seemed the most marvelous thing in the world.

They headed south, Lambert telling her what side streets to take in avoiding downtown. But as Rachel followed his instructions, uneasiness grew in her, dimming the vision of freedom from him. She found herself reviewing their brief stay at her apartment, she being told to turn lights on and off, wash the ash tray, open and close the door. Not just because he wanted to keep the gun on her, she thought, terror closing in on her again. His real concern was with not leaving any fingerprints behind to show that he was ever in her apartment.

If he'd had any idea of letting her live that wouldn't have mattered. He was going to kill her. All his assurances to the contrary meant nothing.

In the shock of admitting to herself that there was no

hope left, Rachel lost control of the car momentarily so that it swerved across the road.

"Hey, watch it!" Lambert exclaimed. "This is my getaway car. I don't want it smashed up."

She brought the car back under control with the *déjà vu* feeling of having had the same experience before.

A moment later she remembered why. She was driving Neil's Corvette home from a party, he too drunk to drive but rousing himself to mumble, "Hey, watch it, Rachel," when she took a curve too fast and almost hit a tree . . .

She knew then what she was going to do. With certain death weighed against possible death it was only a question of choosing the right place.

Her hands tightened on the wheel as they approached the turnoff to Route 1.

Around a curve she found what she was looking for, a big tree standing near the edge of the road. She picked up speed and headed straight toward it.

The last thing she remembered was the tree rushing at her while Lambert, a fraction of a second late in realizing her intent, shouted and tried to grab the wheel.

The next thing she knew she was in a bed. Not her bed. Feeling the side of it with one hand—somehow she couldn't move the other—it seemed too narrow. Then came awareness that she hurt all over.

She opened her eyes trying to orient herself. Why couldn't she move her other hand?

She could move her head a little, enough to see by a shaded light that she was in a hospital room, her left arm in a cast from the shoulder down.

What had happened to her?

Little by little it came back, all of it, up to the moment Lambert had tried to grab the wheel.

What had happened to him?

Presently a nurse appeared. "Oh, you're awake now, Mrs. Carey. How do you feel? Not too good, I reckon."

"No, I don't. What hospital is this?"

"Why, Monmouth Hospital. You were in a car accident."

"I know. What time is it, please?"

"Six in the morning. Nearly daylight. Hear the birds tuning up?"

"There was someone with me—"

"Mr. Lambert. He's still in the recovery room."

"Was he—badly hurt?"

"He'll get better although right now he's a lot worse off than you are. Fractured vertebrae, severe concussion and lacerations from broken glass. He must have been thrown—or thrown himself in front of you—at the time the car hit because you didn't get any cuts to speak of." The nurse paused. "Is there anyone you want notified, Mrs. Carey?"

"My father-in-law and my sister—later," Rachel said drowsily, not feeling equal to facing either of them yet.

"Anything else I can do for you?"

"Not right now, thank you."

"Well then, relax and go back to sleep. I'll look in later." The nurse smiled cheerfully and vanished.

No mention of the gun. Well, that didn't concern her. Rachel, heavily sedated, drifted back to sleep.

The next time she opened her eyes it was nine o'clock and a doctor and a different nurse were standing by her bedside.

The doctor looked at her chart, asked her how she felt and said she'd be good as new in no time.

At ten o'clock Captain Betz arrived. The gun and all that went with it were his concern.

"There's an awful lot for you to sort out," she told him. "Lambert killed Amy and was going to kill me over the letter."

"What letter, Mrs. Carey?"

Rachel sighed as an endless vista of questions opened before her. But at least she was alive to answer them.

She took comfort in that.

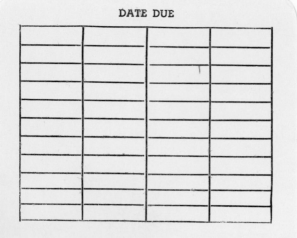